Ellie moved forward until she was only a few paces away from the man she hadn't seen in years, the man she once loved.

"Hello, Arnie." Her mouth as dry as the sandbox at school, she spoke in a voice that was little more than a whisper.

His attention remained focused on her daughter, Torie, for a moment before he lifted his head. He squinted as he looked up at Ellie. There seemed to be no spark of recognition in his eyes.

"I'm sorry my daughter was so forward. I'm afraid she's quite an animal lover." Reaching for Torie, she said, "Give someone else a turn now, honey."

Awareness flickered in his eyes, and he shot the child an assessing look. "Same red hair. I should've known." His voice was as flat as his eyes yet she read an angry denunciation in them.

"It's been a long time."

"Yeah."

Books by Charlotte Carter

Love Inspired

Montana Hearts
Big Sky Reunion
Big Sky Family

CHARLOTTE CARTER

A multipublished author of more than fifty romances, cozy mysteries and inspirational titles, Charlotte Carter lives in Southern California with her husband of forty-nine years and their cat, Mittens. They have two married daughters and five grandchildren. When she's not writing, Charlotte does a little stand-up comedy, "G-Rated Humor for Grownups," and teaches workshops on the craft of writing.

Big Sky Family
Charlotte Carter

LoveInspired

Recycling programs
for this product may
not exist in your area.

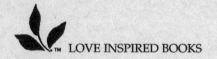 LOVE INSPIRED BOOKS

ISBN-13: 978-0-373-87707-2

BIG SKY FAMILY

www.LoveInspiredBooks.com

Printed in U.S.A.

Then Jesus said to his host,
"When you give a luncheon or dinner,
do not invite your friends, your brothers or sisters,
your relatives, or your rich neighbors; if you do,
they may invite you back and so you will be repaid.
But when you give a banquet, invite the poor,
the crippled, the lame, the blind, and you will be
blessed. Although they cannot repay you, you will
be repaid at the resurrection of the righteous."
—*Luke* 14:12–14

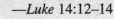

Special thanks to my editor, Emily Rodmell,
who made this book so much better.

Chapter One

Her heart as thick in her throat as if she'd swallowed a ball of yarn, Ellie James drove the van over the cattle guard of the O'Brien ranch. She had once loved the man who had owned the ranch—and had abandoned him eight years ago.

Guilt pressing in on her, Ellie glanced in the rearview mirror and smiled at her six young preschool passengers. She'd been their teacher at Ability Counts Preschool and Day Care Center in Potter Creek, Montana, for a week. She already loved each of the four-year-olds in her class. Three had physical disabilities—cerebral palsy, spina bifida and a prosthetic leg. The remaining three were simply normal kids, including her own daughter, Victoria.

All the youngsters were the best of friends, which proved the value of mainstreaming disabled children early.

"There's horses!" Carson, her spina bifida boy, screamed.

Billy and Shane echoed Carson's high-pitched announcement.

Ellie flinched. "Inside voices, please."

A dozen quarter horses grazed in a beautifully fenced pasture to the right of the drive.

"Carson's getting anxious," her daughter, Torie, said.

"Yes, he is." She glanced at her sparkly eyed, little minx of a daughter, the child's hair almost the same shade of auburn as her own. She counted God's blessings, as she had every day since Torie had been born. "I bet you're excited, too, Torie."

"I wanna ride a great big horse, not a pony."

"We'll have to see what kind of horses they have, honey. And remember, you'll have to take turns with your friends."

Ellie followed her employer's van, filled with another half dozen preschoolers, down the long, dusty drive toward the core of the ranch. Up ahead, the sun glistened off the two-story white farmhouse. The nearby barn appeared sturdy and well maintained, and beyond that a new house was being built, the framing in place.

Her nerves settled a bit. The ranch was not the rundown, shabby place she remembered. Instead, this ranch was a prosperous enterprise.

Surely Arnie O'Brien was gone by now, had moved away, found another life, the ranch sold. The new owners would be the ones who welcomed the preschoolers.

She parked behind the van driven by Vanna Coulter, the owner and founder of Ability Counts. In the corral a mixed group of six saddled horses waited for their young riders.

"All right, children. Let's remember to help our friends." She activated the special lift that would enable Carson to exit in his wheelchair. Anne Marie, who used crutches, stepped onto the lift, as well. Ellie lowered the lift, and the other youngsters exited in a more traditional fashion.

"Hold hands with your partner." The children were so excited, their eyes wide, that she had trouble keeping them together. "Let's see what Miss Vanna has for us."

Her little clutch of youngsters started forward, Torie helping to push Carson's wheelchair. Jefferson, her quietest boy, stayed close to Anne Marie. The morning was already warm, and most of the children were wearing shorts. Ellie suspected by the end of this outing, she'd be happy to trade her lightweight slacks for a pair of shorts, too.

As they reached Vanna and her group of students, a man in a wheelchair rolled out of the barn and came toward them.

Mouth open in stunned disbelief, Ellie watched in amazement as Arnie O'Brien approached.

Each stroke of his hands on the wheels of his chair propelled him forward. The muscles of his darkly tanned forearms flexed and corded. His shoulders were broader than she remembered. Beneath his ebony Stetson, the tips of his silky black hair fluttered in the breeze he created by his sheer strength and power. His sculpted cheekbones and straight nose spoke of his Blackfoot Indian heritage on his mother's side.

A beautiful golden retriever mix trotted along beside him.

"Hey, kids. Who wants to ride a horse?" he called out.

The children sent up a cacophony of "I do! I do!" and raised their hands, waving them in the air.

Torie tugged on Ellie's hand. "Mommy, the man gots a doggy. Can I pet the doggy? Can I?"

"I...I don't know." Her head spun. By coming back to Potter Creek, she'd assumed her path might cross Arnie's again—*if* he was still living in the area. But she'd thought that would be a long shot. To find her former love still at the ranch so many years after his brother's reckless driving had paralyzed and nearly killed Arnie shocked her. She'd expected...

She shook her head. She had no idea what she'd expected.

But she hadn't expected the familiar fluttery feeling around her heart or the sense that she'd given up something special by leaving Potter Creek eight years ago. No matter that Arnie, barely out of a medically induced coma, had told her to leave. To go away. She'd deserted him when he most needed her. She'd broken the trust they'd had in each other.

Torie broke away from the group. She made a dash for Arnie and his dog.

Before Ellie could call her back, Torie slid to a stop right in front of Arnie.

"Hey, mister, can I pet your doggy? I love doggies. Does he like little girls? Can I pet him, huh?"

Arnie quirked his lips into a half smile. "Everyone can pet Sheila, but you have to do it one at a time. Okay?"

Not waiting for additional encouragement, Torie squatted down in front of Sheila, who sat calmly while the child stroked her head and ran her fingers through her golden coat.

"She's bea-u-tiful," Torie crooned.

The other children edged forward. Ellie moved with them until she was only a few paces away from Arnie. Unconsciously, she fingered the silver cross she wore around her neck, a gift from her father the year she graduated from eighth grade. Only after Torie was born and Ellie had made her peace with the Lord had she begun to wear it again.

"Hello, Arnie." Her mouth as dry as the sandbox at school, she spoke in a voice that was little more than a whisper.

His attention remained focused on Torie for a moment before he lifted his head. He squinted as he looked up at Ellie. There seemed to be no spark of recognition in his eyes. Only a blank stare.

"I'm sorry my daughter was so forward. I'm afraid she's quite an animal lover." Reaching for Torie, she said, "Give someone else a turn now, honey."

Awareness flickered in his eyes, and he shot the child an assessing look. "Same red hair. I should've known." His voice was as flat as his eyes, yet she read an angry denunciation in them.

"It's been a long time," she said.

"Yeah." No smile. A single word in bitter acknowledgment.

The sting of his response forced her to look away. She had no reason to expect anything more, but it still hurt. "Who wants to pet Sheila next? Remember to be gentle."

She drew Torie to her side, a protective hand on her daughter's shoulder.

"Sheila's a very nice doggy, Mommy. Maybe someday we could have a doggy, too?"

"We'll see."

As Carson approached Sheila in his wheelchair, Arnie's brows tugged together in apparent confusion. He glanced back at Ellie.

"Why are you here?" he asked.

"I'm teaching at Ability Counts Preschool. I started this week. Four-year-olds."

"That's ironic, isn't it?"

Before she could explain how she'd worked hard to earn her degree in early childhood education and added an elementary school teaching credential to her résumé, Arnie's younger brother, Daniel, sauntered out of the barn. Easily recognizable with his long legs and the cocky way he wore his hat on the back of his head, he called to the youngsters.

"Hey, what's taking you guys so long? Isn't anybody planning to go riding today?"

Instantly, the children lost interest in Sheila. They walked, ran and wheeled their way to the barn. In a quick maneuver, Arnie turned his wheelchair around and drove purposely after them.

Vanna and Ellie followed more slowly. A woman in her late sixties, Vanna stood nearly six feet tall and wore her gray hair closely cropped. But it was her smile and obvious love for all "her children" that endeared her to those who attended the preschool as well as their parents.

"The two young men hosting us have been a wonderful help to the school," Vanna said. "Arnie's on our board of directors, a very valuable resource. He's also on the Bozeman Paralympics board. He's trying to start a regional program to train local teenagers with physical disabilities for Western riding events. All the organization offers currently are English-style equestrian events, which leaves some of our kids without an event that appeals to them."

At some level, Ellie wasn't surprised that Arnie was involved with programs for people with disabilities. Of the two brothers, Arnie had been the serious, solid one, often at odds with his wilder, more rambunctious brother.

As a nineteen-year-old, Ellie had been stretching her wings, ready to try anything, while Arnie generally watched with amusement as she tried to break her neck with some half-baked stunt Daniel had cooked up.

Arnie, in his quiet way, had given her balance when

she needed it. She hadn't had that anymore when she first moved away to Spokane, to her regret.

Arnie and Daniel separated the two groups of youngsters. Daniel took his clutch of four-year-olds into the corral to ride, while Arnie lined up his kids for a lesson in grooming horses.

Needing to keep her distance from Arnie, not wanting to feel that tingle of excitement or the slashing pain of guilt, Ellie followed Daniel into the corral. He introduced the children to Marc, an older teenager who would assist the kids.

Daniel turned to Ellie. "If you can help out, that'd be..." He stopped midsentence and frowned. "Ellie?"

At his recognition, her first smile since she arrived at the ranch lifted her lips. "The bad penny has returned."

"Hey, no, it's great you're back." He glanced toward the barn and frowned. He hesitated. "Does Arnie know?"

"Yes, we've said hello." Barely. His greeting had been less than enthusiastic, which she should have expected.

With the ease of a working cowboy, Daniel picked up Carson and hefted him into a special saddle on a sorrel. He began securing the grinning boy so he couldn't fall off. "Yeah, well, that's Arnie for you. The quiet brother. I know who'll really be glad to see you again."

"Who's that?" Most of her high school friends had moved away, and she'd lost track of them.

He instructed Carson to sit tight until everyone had mounted. "Mindy. You know, Aunt Martha's grandniece? She's Mindy O'Brien now." He stood a little taller, and his chest puffed out with pride.

Ellie's eyes popped open and her jaw dropped. "You married Mindy?" A couple of years older than Ellie, Mindy had helped her learn to knit one long-ago summer, when Mindy was visiting her aunt.

"Yep. Tied the knot last spring." He bent a little closer to her. "We're expecting a baby come the end of the year."

She gasped with delight and covered her mouth with her hand. "Oh, that's wonderful! We were friends only that one summer, but I remember her well." She glanced around. "Is she here now?"

"Nope. She manages Aunt Martha's Knitting and Notions shop. She'll be back in time for supper."

Daniel moved on to boost Torie into the saddle of a buckskin who'd been waiting patiently for a rider. Her skinny, bare legs poked almost straight out to the sides.

"What's my horse's name?" Torie asked.

"This is Patches. He'll take real good care of you."

"I like Patches!"

As Ellie helped Shane mount, she promised herself she'd stop by the knitting shop as soon as she could find the time. It'd be great to see Mindy again. She certainly hadn't expected her friend to return to Potter Creek after she'd gone back to Pittsburgh without saying goodbye to anyone.

Then again, when Ellie left Potter Creek, she hadn't expected to return home to stay, either.

But fate—and in Ellie's case, a good dose of stupidity—

had changed the best-laid plans. An unintended pregnancy plus a man who had no intention in being a father changed a lot in a woman's life.

She sincerely prayed this current change was one for the better.

Chapter Two

Talk about being skewered by a wild bull!

That evening on the back porch of the ranch house, Arnie forked the three T-bone steaks he'd barbecued onto a serving platter. He'd spent the better part of the afternoon thinking about Ellie James and how she'd showed up out of nowhere. He could've been knocked over by a newborn calf.

She taught handicapped kids.

She'd walked out on him after the accident, unable to face life with a cripple. *Probably a good decision,* he admitted. *The best thing for her. But not for him,* he thought selfishly.

Was she living some sort of a twisted penance now? Forcing herself to care for those who repulsed her?

She had a daughter, a beautiful sprite of a child with Ellie's lush red hair that captured sunbeams and the same hint of freckles across her nose.

Where was her husband? The child's father?

Arnie had no answers to his questions and assured himself that he didn't want any. Ancient history. Better to leave it that way.

Daniel pushed open the screen door. "Hey, bro, Mindy's got the salad and rolls on the table. Are we gonna eat those steaks sometime tonight, or are you gonna let Sheila scarf 'em down all by herself?"

"I'm coming." With the serving platter across his lap, he rolled into the kitchen. Always his faithful companion, Sheila was right beside him, her toenails clicking on the tile. She'd get her share of steak on the bone he'd give her after dinner.

"Oh, those look delicious." Mindy was already seated at the round oak table, the same table where Arnie and Daniel had eaten since their childhood. The same table where their drunken father had yelled and railed at them for no particular reason and had sometimes slapped them silly.

Daniel, a rebel at heart, had always gotten the worst of it.

But those days were long gone, and even better days lay ahead.

Blonde and blue-eyed, Mindy had had a certain glow about her since she'd married Daniel. That glow had blossomed even more once she discovered she was pregnant. Having lost a child from her first marriage, she cherished the new life growing in her.

A stab of envy zinged Arnie right in his solar plexus. Why did Ellie have to come back to Potter Creek, reminding him of all the things he'd never have, like a wife and children of his own?

He selected a steak for himself, put it on his plate and passed the platter to Mindy.

"I don't know what I'm going to do when you move into your new house," Mindy said. "You'd better promise to come here for dinner every night."

"You only say that because you want me to be your kitchen slave," Arnie teased.

She laughed. "Never a slave. A highly valued chef is closer to the truth. And a great brother-in-law," she added.

"I vote for the slave part." Daniel plopped the third steak on his plate.

Arnie snorted. He reached for Daniel's hand and Mindy's, and they linked hands with each other. Arnie bowed his head. "Dear Lord, thank You once again for the food You have provided. Bless us and keep us safe, including little Rumpelstiltskin, who's growing in Mindy's tummy. Amen."

Choking, Mindy grabbed for her glass of water. "We're not going to name our baby Rumpelstiltskin!" she croaked.

"Well, you'd better come up with something better pretty soon." Cutting into his steak, he gave Mindy a wink. "Uncle Arnie is growing quite fond of little Rumple."

Laughing, she shook her head.

They ate in comfortable silence for a while; then Daniel asked Mindy, "How was the shop today?"

"Busy for a Friday. The knitting and needlepoint club is getting ready for the church's Autumn Craft Fair. All the ladies want to have items to sell to help raise money for the church. Baby caps and sweaters are the most popular for the knitters. I had to place a new order for baby yarn this afternoon."

"Sounds good. My wife, the entrepreneur." Daniel forked another bite of meat into his mouth and talked around it. "Hey, I forgot to tell you. Ellie James is back in town."

For a frozen moment, Arnie held his knife poised over his steak.

"Ellie? I remember her," Mindy said. "Is she here to stay or just visiting her mother?"

"I guess she's here to stay. She's got a job with the preschool that comes out for Friday riding lessons. She was with them this morning."

Mindy turned to Arnie. "She was such a fun person. So energetic I could barely keep up with her. She used to hang out with your crowd."

Keeping his eyes focused on his dinner, Arnie nodded as he cut his steak. "Yeah, she hung out with us." And as she got older, she wasn't just hanging out. Mindy had been gone before Ellie and he had become a couple. She wouldn't have known how Ellie had kicked the possibility of a future together to the curb when she cut out for Spokane.

"Well, isn't that interesting?" Mindy's suddenly chirpy, singsong voice grated on Arnie's nerves. "Maybe we can all get together again. It'd be fun to double-date sometime."

He turned on Mindy, glaring at her, his pulse thundering in his ears. "That's not gonna happen. Not ever."

Just because Ellie had moved back to Potter Creek did not mean he had to see her. Or think about her. Or remember the numbing pain in his chest he'd lived with since she left.

Nope. He intended to stay far away from Ellie James.

He imagined she felt the same way about him.

The house where Ellie grew up, just outside of Potter Creek, was a one-story white farmhouse with bedrooms added onto the back, a covered porch along the front and a mudroom stuck onto one side like a wart. A detached, oversize garage and workshop had served to shelter farm equipment, and a small barn and corral had once housed Ellie's horse, Samson, but had remained unused for years.

After Ellie's father died two years ago, her mother had leased out all the surrounding farmland, retaining only the one acre where the house and outbuildings stood.

With a sigh of relief to be home, Ellie parked her compact car near the side entrance. As she had expected, the first week of school had been a challenging one.

Seeing Arnie this morning had been even more difficult.

He hadn't been at all pleased to see her. Anger had

simmered right below the surface of his detached manner toward her. *Rightfully so,* she admitted.

She'd been the one to leave. *She'd* started a new life hundreds of miles away. *She'd* felt so guilty about what she had done, she'd made some foolish mistakes.

None of which meant she had forgotten Arnie.

He'd told her to leave more than once.

Torie popped open the back door of the car. "I gotta tell Grandma BarBar about my horse." Slamming the door closed, she raced up the steps and into the house to relate her adventures to her grandmother Barbara.

Briefcase in hand, Ellie followed at a more leisurely pace.

"…rode a horse named Patches around and around. I kept saying 'Giddy up,' but the man wouldn't let Patches run fast." Torie paused only briefly to take a breath. "Then another man gave us brushes, and we brushed and brushed a horse. The horse was very dusty. That made Carson sneeze."

Sitting in the kitchen, at the long white-pine table, Grandma BarBar listened to Torie's tale, nodding where appropriate and making encouraging noises. A little overweight, Barbara wore wire-rimmed glasses, and her hair had lost most of the auburn color it once had. The permed curls were nearly all gray.

Ellie set her briefcase on the counter and idly checked the day's mail, which her mother **had dropped** in the woven basket.

"The man with the brushes showed us how to clean the icky stuff out of the horse's hoof. He had a doggy he let me pet, and he said he had to sit in a wheelchair all the time 'cause his legs didn't work anymore. I told him Carson's legs didn't work, either, but I still liked him."

Barbara lifted her head. "Ellen? Where did the school take the children to ride?"

Without glancing toward her mother, Ellie tucked a wayward strand of hair behind her ear. "Turns out it was the O'Brien ranch. I'd been so busy all week, I hadn't thought to ask Vanna where we were going."

"The man in the wheelchair was real nice, Mommy."

"Yes, honey, I know." Ellie returned the mail to the basket. Bills and a newsletter from the agricultural extension service were of no interest to her.

"It was Arnie O'Brien, wasn't it?" Barbara said, a stunned expression on her face.

A guilty flush warmed Ellie's cheeks. "Yes, Arnie was helping the children. So was his brother. Daniel's married now, and they're expecting a baby."

"Mommy, if I learn to ride a horse really, really, really good, can I have my very own horse? Please, can I? I would loooove to have my own horse."

"I'm sure you would, honey. But horses are expensive and take a lot of care." Working in the child care business was not exactly a lucrative profession, though it should be. What made it ideal for Ellie was the opportunity to work with mainstreamed handicapped kids and live at home with her mother, mostly rent-free. Being near her mother, who'd been depressed since she'd become a widow, was an added bonus. Ellie hoped having an exuberant child around would lift her spirits.

"We could ask the man in the wheelchair to come take care of my horse. He was very nice."

Ellie swallowed hard. *Not a good plan, sweetie.*

"Little Miss Chatterbox," Barbara said, "why don't you go wash up? It's almost supper time, and I want to talk with your mother."

Torie's slender shoulders slumped. "I know. You want to talk about grown-up things."

"Go on, Torie," Ellie said, although she wasn't eager to pursue the topic her mother no doubt had in mind. "Wash your hands and face, and don't forget to use soap."

Skipping and hopping, Torie did as she'd been told.

"I'd better go clean up, too," Ellie said, eager to avoid any discussion about Arnie.

"I do hope you won't be taking up with that young man again."

Ellie bristled. "No worries on that score, Mother. I doubt that he'd be interested." Her actions eight years ago had shut that door permanently. Actions her mother had advised and encouraged.

"Just as well," Barbara sniffed.

After Arnie's accident, Ellie's mother had encouraged Ellie to move away from Arnie. Barbara's brother, Bob, had been born with cerebral palsy and was severely handicapped. Watching a loved one suffer pain and humiliation haunted Barbara. She didn't want her daughter to endure the same difficult experience.

To her shame and regret, her mother's constant concern about Arnie's future had added to Ellie's ultimate decision to leave Potter Creek and move to Spokane.

The first of a long litany of mistakes she'd made that had changed her life.

With the Lord's help, she'd turned her life around. But that didn't mean that a proud man like Arnie would ever be able to forgive her for turning her back on him.

Early Saturday morning, a gang of volunteer construction workers showed up at the O'Brien ranch. Most of the guys were from Potter Creek Community Church. As the half-dozen pickups pulled to a stop, Arnie rolled out to meet them.

"I've got a big pot of coffee ready," he announced. "And Daniel went into town early for fresh doughnuts. Help yourselves."

Like a pack of ravenous chowhounds, the men gathered around the coffeepot on what would someday be Arnie's back porch. Their wives and girlfriends would show up around noontime with picnic baskets full of lunch makings. Building his new house was like an old-fashioned barn raising, and he was grateful for every bit of help he got.

Since Daniel had announced he was going to marry Mindy, Arnie had planned to move out of the old ranch house and into his own home. Now that Mindy was expecting, providing his brother and his wife some extra space was even more important.

Given the cost of construction, bringing the plan to

fruition would have been impossible without the help of his friends. In fact, half the community had lent a hand in one way or another.

Coffee and doughnut in hand, Tim Johnson, a licensed contractor and good friend, sauntered over to Arnie. "We're gonna start putting up the exterior plywood sheathing today. If that goes well, next week we could be adding the siding."

"That's terrific, Tim. You know how much I appreciate your help. All the guys' help."

"No problem. If the situation was reversed, you'd be there for us."

"I'd sure try to be." But Arnie knew he'd never have a chance to return the favor, at least not in the same way.

"I got my chimney guy to say he'd come next week so we can get the flashings in before the siding goes up. He's giving you a good price."

"Thanks, Tim. I appreciate it." One of the lessons he'd learned after the accident was that he'd never be as independent as he had been before. For some things, he'd have to rely on others. That had been a hard truth to swallow, and it still didn't go down real smoothly.

Daniel came striding across the distance from the barn, a tool belt around his waist. Apparently he had finished mucking out the horse stalls and was ready to go to work on the house.

"Hey, you guys," Daniel said to the men still hanging around the coffeepot. "You can't stand around drinking coffee and eatin' doughnuts all day. We gotta get this house sealed up tight before the first snow flies."

"Yeah, yeah. We know, Danny boy."

"Hey, who made you the boss?"

Amid a lot of friendly joshing and gently barbed comments, the men set to work. Guys grunted as they lifted heavy loads of plywood. Hammers banged nails home. Orders were shouted out. Power saws whined.

The heat of the day rose. Sweat darkened the back of the men's shirts and dripped from their chins.

Arnie wheeled his chair up the temporary ramp into his living room and looked around. His pride, his gratitude, were tempered by the knowledge that he'd never share this house with someone who could be his partner in making it a home.

A sense of betrayal rose bitter in his throat.

Ellie!

Even knowing she'd done the right thing to leave him, he couldn't quite accept that the woman who had cried at his bedside and held his hand for five solid days after the accident had actually walked out of his life. She hadn't stayed to fight for their love.

Now she was back.

And he couldn't stop thinking about her.

Chapter Three

The white steeple soared above Potter Creek Community Church, glistening in the morning sunlight, a beacon of hope and a promise of the Lord's love.

Holding her daughter's hand, Ellie followed the path to the building that housed Sunday school classrooms. She'd grown up attending this church, and now her daughter would enjoy the same experience.

Somewhere between her sixteenth birthday, when she decided her friends were far more fun to be with than attending church, and her surprise pregnancy at age twenty-one, Ellie had lost her faith. Or, more accurately, she had simply ignored the teachings of the Lord.

Nothing like realizing you were going to be a single parent to drag a woman back into the folds of the church. That and praying for forgiveness of her sins.

"Will I know anybody in my Sunday school class?" Wearing a summery dress and her shiny Mary Jane shoes, Torie stretched her little legs in order to step over the cracks in the sidewalk.

"We'll have to see, honey."

Ellie introduced herself and Torie to the teacher. In less than two minutes, Torie was playing with the other children in the class.

Kissing her daughter goodbye, she went in search of her mother, who was saving her a seat.

Off to the side of the main entrance a group of churchgoers had gathered around a table. The banner on the wall behind the table read Support Paralympics.

Ellie's steps slowed. Her mouth dried. As though she had no control over her own feet, they angled her directly toward the table and the person she instinctively knew would be sitting there.

As she drew closer, the two men who had been blocking her view stepped aside. Arnie spotted her the moment the men moved away. His dark eyes flared momentarily before he could shutter them and coax his expression into one of disinterest. His short-sleeved sport shirt revealed the deeply tanned column of his neck and his muscular arms.

"Looks like you're all dressed up for church," he said.

Ellie's tongue swept across her dry lips. "Yes. I just left Torie in the child-care room."

"I didn't know you ever went to church."

"I don't remember you as a regular churchgoer, either."

"Good point. Having a near-death experience forces a guy to take a look at his life, make some changes."

"Having a baby out of wedlock does the same thing." She cringed, wondering what Arnie would think of her. Wondering if he would condemn her for sleeping with a man outside the sanctity of marriage.

His brows lifted slowly but not in condemnation. "No husband?"

She held herself very still. "Turned out he wasn't interested in being a daddy." Or a husband, for that matter. Foolishly, she'd given herself too easily to a man who couldn't or wouldn't cherish her.

A small V formed between his brows. "Torie's a cute kid. He's missing something special."

She smiled, and some of the tension that had kept her nerves as taut as a piano wire eased. "I think so, too."

"So do you want to be one of my sponsors?" He shoved a glossy brochure across the table to her. "I'm trying to raise a couple of thousand dollars for the Bozeman Paralympics organization. We're hosting a marathon race in a couple of weeks, and I've entered the wheelchair division. I want them to start a Western riding event. You know, cow cutting and trail riding. Events like that. The money will help them do that."

"Sure, I'll sponsor you. Vanna said something about you working with the Paralympics group."

"A couple of years ago some guys in the organization dragged me to Bridger Bowl outside of Bozeman and took me skiing." He handed her a pledge form.

"Skiing? How could you—"

"I'm on a wheelchair basketball team, too. We won the regionals last year." He lifted his chin, challenging her to question him.

"Congratulations." Her admiration for all he had overcome kicked up a notch.

"Paralympics is like Ability Counts Preschool. It's not your disabilities that matter, only your abilities."

She heard chastisement in his voice and knew she deserved the rebuke. She opened her mouth to apologize, but he stopped her.

"The prelude's started. We better get inside." He put some paperweights on the stack of brochures and pledge forms. "You can bring that back to me after church, if you're still interested."

"Of course."

He wheeled out from behind the table and gestured for her to precede him inside, a gentlemanly courtesy. She stepped in front of him, fully aware that he was right behind her. His eyes were on her, his unseen gaze raising her temperature, sending a rush of heat to her face and a wave of guilt to her conscience. Her hand shaking slightly, she took a program from the greeter at the door.

Why on earth had she walked right up to his table? She'd vowed to steer clear of the man. With a firm grip on the church program, she promised she wouldn't forget again.

She spotted her mother in a pew halfway down the first aisle and slid in beside her.

"Did you have problems with Torie?" Barbara whispered.

"No, she's fine."

"What took you so long?"

"I, uh, stopped to talk with someone I knew," Ellie hedged.

"Oh, that's nice, dear."

Pastor Redmond, who looked to be in his fifties, stepped out onto the stage and raised his arms, asking the congregation to rise for the first hymn.

Fumbling for the hymnal, Ellie dropped her program and the pledge form Arnie had given her. Barbara bent to pick them up.

The organist played the first few bars of "Just a Closer Walk with Thee;" then the congregation and choir joined in.

Barbara nudged Ellie with her elbow and handed her back the pledge form. "With a daughter to raise, I didn't imagine you had extra money to give away. I don't think it's a good idea for you to get involved with him again."

Ellie's face flamed hot. Her jaw clenched, and she put the pledge form on the pew beside her.

Other than being a paraplegic, there was nothing wrong with Arnie O'Brien. He was trying to support a worthwhile organization, a worthwhile cause.

In Ellie's view, that made him more able-bodied and *worthwhile* than the good-time Charlie who had impregnated her and then deserted her, leaving her to raise their child alone. She should have steered clear of Jake Radigan.

Just as she should stay clear of Arnie now, but for a far different reason.

Before his accident, Arnie O'Brien would never have deserted a woman or his child. That nobility, that sense of responsibility, hadn't changed simply because he was confined to a wheelchair.

She believed that with all of her heart.

In contrast, Ellie had walked away from the man she'd loved. Scarcely the action of a noble woman. Rather the foolish action of a nineteen-year-old girl.

Propelled by her anger at her mother, and maybe at her own mindless decisions, Ellie scribbled in a larger pledge amount for the Paralympics than she could strictly afford and wrote a check on the spot.

After the church service ended, she ducked out the side door while her mother waited to speak to the minister. She hurried to retrieve Torie from her classroom and returned to find Arnie back at his table, raking in more pledges from his friends.

"Look, Mommy. Arnie's here!" Breaking away from Ellie, Torie beelined it across the patio to Arnie's table. Instead of stopping in front of the table, she squeezed in behind it, next to Arnie.

Sheila stood, backing away from her spot next to Arnie to avoid being stepped on by Torie. Arnie leaned back in his chair, equally startled by child's sudden arrival. "Hey, squirt. What's up?"

"I want to ask you an im-por-tant question."

He glanced toward Ellie, his lips twitching with the threat of a smile. "Sure, ask away."

Torie's face scrunched into its most serious expression. "If my mommy bought me a horse of my very, very own, would you come take care of it for me?"

Ellie choked. "Victoria James! You're not supposed to—"

"I don't know, squirt," Arnie said with equal seriousness. "That would be a big job to take care of a horse."

"I know, and I'm too little. I get a dollar a week allowance. I could pay you that much."

By now those standing around Arnie's table were fully engaged in the conversation, to Ellie's mortification.

"High time you earned an honest dollar, Arnie," a man said.

"Isn't she cute?" a woman said. "I bet when she's a teenager, her father will have to guard the door and lock the windows to keep the boys out."

Ellie had heard enough. "Come on, Torie. We have to find Grandma."

"But Arnie hasn't said he'll take care of my horse yet."

"You don't have a horse, so why don't we worry about who's going to take care of it if and when you have one?" With an apologetic smile, she handed the pledge form and check to Arnie.

He glanced at the form and the check, then looked up at Ellie. "Preschool teachers must earn more than I realized."

"No such luck, but a guilty conscience can make a person feel generous."

"No need for you to feel guilty."

That was nice of him to say, but she knew it was a lie.

He held up the check. "Don't you want to hold off on this in case I don't actually finish the race?"

"You'll finish. I don't doubt that for a moment." She took Torie's hand. "Tell Arnie goodbye, honey. Grandma's waiting for us."

With her daughter in tow, Ellie hurried toward the parking lot. Having such an outgoing child had its disadvantages.

A muscle pulsed in Arnie's jaw as he watched Ellie and her daughter scurry away. His hands grasped the armrests of his chair, turning his knuckles white.

He had to get a grip on his volatile emotions—a boiling mix of anger, longing and grief—whenever Ellie showed up.

In eight long years he still hadn't figured out how to do that.

Chapter Four

"Shane, we don't throw sand at our friends." Ellie quickly corrected the boy's behavior Monday morning, during outdoor playtime at the preschool.

It was the second week of classes, and she already felt more comfortable with her students, knew all their names and their differing personalities.

They seemed more at ease with her, as well.

On this hot September day, most of the children wore shorts and a T-shirt, their arms and legs darkly tanned from a summer in the sun.

Squinting, Ellie scanned the play yard to check on her other students just as a van pulled into the parking area. A moment later, Arnie rode the wheelchair lift down to the ground. Sheila hopped right off and waited for him.

Ellie's heart stuttered an extra beat and her breathing accelerated. She wondered what had brought Arnie to the school.

Some of the children recognized him and his dog.

They raced to the wire fence, shouting his name. Torie was there first.

"Arnie! Arnie! Did you bring your horses?" she cried.

"Not today, squirt." He reached through the fence to tweak Torie's nose. "Hey, kids, you having a good time at school?"

They clamored to answer him all at once, a chorus of high-pitched, excited voices.

Without giving it any thought, Ellie strolled toward the fence and Arnie. He looked dressed for wrangling cows, well-worn, faded jeans, blue work shirt and black Stetson firmly in place. Despite the wheelchair, he managed to radiate sinewy strength, constrained only by his self-confidence.

"Good morning." Her voice a little husky, she forced a smile. "I hope my check didn't bounce already."

His lips twitched, and a sparkle appeared in his dark eyes. "No one has deposited it yet. Should I be worried?"

"No, of course not," she gasped. "I just thought—"

"I came by to see Vanna. There's a school board meeting Thursday night. They're going to vote on Vanna's request to turn Ability Counts into a charter school, kindergarten through third grade."

"Yes, Vanna mentioned that to me." Vanna's dream of expanding Ability Counts from four preschool classrooms to a school for all primary grades was a big reason Ellie had been so eager to accept the job here. The school board hearing was a first step.

"I'm going speak to the need for specialized services for disabled kids. I wanted to touch base with her before the meeting, and I was in town, anyway."

"I think she's in the office."

"Good. See you later, kids." He started to roll up the ramp, then stopped. "Are you coming to the board meeting?"

"Yes. Vanna wanted as many supporters as possible to attend. We've asked all the parents to be there if they can."

He held her gaze for a moment, making Ellie wonder if he was pleased or dismayed by her answer. Then he nodded. "I'll see you Thursday night."

He wheeled away, Sheila trotting along with him. Ellie exhaled. After all these years, he shouldn't have any effect on her. No racing pulse. No shallow breathing. No ache for what might have been.

But he did affect her. Like a direct shot of caffeine into her veins. A shot she'd better get over soon, before she made a fool of herself.

"All right, children," she said, shaking off the image of Arnie's muscular arms and his sweet smile for the kids. "Let's go inside for story time. Can you all please line up at the door?" She gently herded the youngsters toward the classroom.

Before she had the children settled down, Peggy Numark appeared at the classroom door. Short and petite, Peggy looked like a pixie and would never be taken for the fifty-year-old teacher that she was. More like a mother of one of the children.

"Ellie, Vanna would like to see you in the conference room. She asked me to take your kids for a few minutes."

Ellie frowned. "Now?"

Without any further explanation, Peggy said, "Come along, children. Miss Peggy has the best story she's going to read to you."

Dutifully, the children trailed after the energetic teacher.

With a puzzled shake of her head, Ellie headed for the conference room, located near Vanna's office. She arrived to find Arnie still meeting with Vanna.

Ellie slowed her pace. "Peggy said you wanted—"

"Yes, come in, please." Vanna waved her in the door. "I need to pick your brain a bit."

"She already picked mine," Arnie said, deadpan. "And discovered it was empty."

Ellie's lips twitched. "That's hard to believe."

"Not when you know I spend my days talking to a dog and a bunch of cows," he countered.

Sheila shook her head, rattling her collar, as though she disagreed with Arnie's statement.

Choosing a chair opposite Arnie, Ellie sat down at the long table. "What did you need?" she asked Vanna.

"I want it to be obvious to the school board members at the meeting Thursday that we have a lot of support in the community," Vanna said. "I'm not quite sure how to do that in a subtle, but very visible, way."

"I suggested everyone could wave little American

flags," Arnie said. "I think Nate at the grocery store probably has some."

"I'm not keen on that idea. Not specific enough." Vanna's brows lowered in thought, and she rubbed her left arm.

"Maybe a campaign-style button," Ellie said. "Something big enough to be seen at a distance, with Ability Counts printed on it."

Vanna brightened. "Well, now…" She turned to Arnie. "What do you think?"

"I've always thought Ellie was more than just a beautiful woman. She's smart, too." His steady gaze latched onto hers, but he didn't smile.

For a moment, Ellie couldn't breathe. Was that what he'd really thought of her? Could that possibly still be true? It was impossible to read his thoughts when he sent such a mixed message.

Vanna eyed Arnie with interest and smiled. "Then I'd say we have a winner. Can you find out where to get those buttons made?" she asked Ellie.

"I may have to drive to Manhattan, but a copier store should be able to do the job."

"Perfect," Vanna announced.

She stood to end the meeting, and Ellie followed suit, still hearing the echo of Arnie's words in her head. *Beautiful and smart.*

After school, Ellie drove the ten miles to Manhattan. She made the arrangements for the buttons to be ready in time for the meeting, then decided to stop on the way home to say hello to Mindy at her shop in Potter Creek.

"How come we're going to a knitting store?" Torie asked.

"A friend of mine works there. I want to say hello to her and have her meet you." Ellie checked the rearview mirror and eased out of her parking spot.

"Does she have any kids I can play with?"

"I'm afraid not." Reversing direction, she drove out of the parking lot and turned west, toward the center of Potter Creek. The small town served a population of maybe five thousand people in the surrounding area. For any major shopping excursion, the locals drove to Manhattan, or all the way to Bozeman. "Maybe she'll have some yarn crafts you'd like to make."

"Are you going to buy some yarn to make me something?"

"I might. You could use a new sweater for fall."

Main Street looked much like it always had: grocery, hardware and drugstore on one side of the street; a diner, real estate and newspaper offices on the opposite side. At the far end of town, a brick building served as city hall and was adjacent to the popular public swimming pool. A stark contrast to downtown Spokane or even to the suburbs of that sprawling, big city with its traffic congestion and the press of a growing population.

To its advantage, however, Potter Creek was a size that a person could get her brain wrapped around, a comfortable, friendly place to live. Schoolkids rode their bikes on Main Street, and neighbors caught up with local news while lingering in front of the grocery store.

Home, Ellie thought. She'd stayed away too long.

She pulled up in front of Aunt Martha's Knitting and Notions. The front window featured posters of class offerings and autumn specials on wool yarn. A cute knitted vest adorned a clear-plastic mannequin.

"We're here," Ellie announced. "Out you go."

Dozens of memories flooded Ellie. Aunt Martha teaching her to knit, despite Ellie's initial lack of enthusiasm. Making friends with Mindy, dragging her into attempting new things, like floating down the river on a homemade wooden raft. When the raft fell apart, they both nearly drowned. The ever-responsible Arnie had to rescue them.

A frown tugged at her forehead. The reckless driving accident with his brother behind the wheel had stolen so much from Arnie, not just the use of his legs, but his self-image, as well. Adjusting to his new circumstances had to have been difficult.

Guilt tightened a knot in her stomach. *You should have stayed to help him,* she thought.

Holding Torie's hand, Ellie stepped inside the small knitting shop, setting off tiny wind chimes above the door.

"Oh, my..." she murmured. Over the years the shop had been upgraded and was chock-full of merchandise. In addition to bins of all types of yarn, one whole corner area displayed needle-craft samples and bins of thread in every color imaginable.

Mindy appeared from a back room. "Ellie? It's you, isn't it!" Arms open wide, she rushed forward to embrace Ellie. "Oh, my goodness. Daniel said you were back in town, but I wasn't home when you came to the ranch and I missed seeing you at church. I'm so glad you dropped by."

"I had to check out my old haunts, right?" One of those smiles that comes from the heart and lightens your spirits lifted Ellie's lips. "I can't believe the changes you've made to the shop. And by the way, I understand double congratulations are in order, Mrs. O'Brien, on your marriage and your pregnancy."

A quick flush colored Mindy's cheeks as she laughed. With her blond hair and fair complexion, blushing had once been the bane of her existence, particularly when Daniel had flirted with her.

"And this must be your daughter Daniel was telling me about," Mindy said. "I understand she wants a horse of her own."

"I'm afraid that's not in our immediate future. Victoria, say hello to Mrs. O'Brien."

"Hello." Torie shook hands with Mindy. "Do you like horses, too?"

"I certainly do. My husband raises some of the finest quarter horses in the whole state."

Torie put on her most serious expression. "Maybe someday my mommy could buy a horse from you."

Ellie hooked her arm around her daughter's shoulders and gave her an affectionate squeeze. "I'm afraid Torie's a bit fixated on horses these days."

"Most kids around here are."

"I told Torie you might have some craft projects suitable for her."

Mindy brightened. "I do. I'll be getting more in before Christmas, but come see what I have now." She took Torie's hand and walked her to the back of the shop.

Ellie followed. When she was living in Spokane, working full-time as a waitress and taking as many college classes as she could manage, plus caring for Torie, it had been hard to make friends.

Coming back to Potter Creek meant she'd have more time and have the chance to renew old friendships. Perhaps that was what coming home was all about.

"Do you run the shop all by yourself?" Ellie asked.

"Mostly. Sometimes Aunt Martha fills in for an afternoon or two to give me a break, and I have Ivy from the diner stand in for me occasionally."

Ellie frowned. "How are you going to handle things after the baby arrives?"

She smiled brightly. "Oh, I may close down for a few weeks. Then I'll bring him or her along with me. That should work for the first year or so."

"Watch out for those toddler years," Ellie warned, thinking her friend might not fully realize what an energy drain a child could be. "There's no keeping them corralled in a playpen then."

"I suppose you're right," Mindy conceded.

While Ellie and Mindy caught up with their respective lives Torie searched through the assortment of craft possibilities.

"So, um, where's Torie's father?" Mindy asked.

"I haven't a clue. Apparently, being a father wasn't on his to-do list." Jake Radigan hadn't been a college student, but he'd hung out with some of the guys, showing off his motorcycle, revving the engine. Apparently he was a good mechanic, because he kept his friends' junker cars running, working out of a garage behind his rental house.

His "wild side" had attracted Ellie, she supposed. His lack of roots.

That same lack of roots meant that he rode off into the sunset on his bike virtually the moment he learned Ellie was pregnant.

In retrospect, that was probably for the best.

Torie returned from her search in the back of the shop with an "Old Woman in a Shoe" craft that she could lace with red yarn and hang on her bedroom wall.

"I found some yarn that would make a pretty sweater for me," Torie announced.

"Well, then, let's take a look." Ellie followed her daughter to a wall filled with bins of yarn. Mindy joined them.

Torie held up a skein of emerald-green sport-weight yarn. "The green goes with my eyes."

"Yes, it does, sweetie," Mindy announced.

Ellie thought so, too. The pale green eyes were the only trace of Torie's father she saw in her daughter.

"All right, honey. We'll have to pick out a pattern you like." During the evenings, sitting with her mother, watching TV, would be a good time to knit.

After pouring over pattern books and making a selection, Ellie was paying for their purchases when Mindy said, "You'll both have to come out to the ranch for supper one day soon."

Credit card in hand, Ellie stiffened. "Oh, I don't know."

"You must. My favorite brother-in-law is the best cook in the world. He and Daniel remodeled the kitchen years ago, so it's totally accessible for him. You should taste his chili." She brought her fingertips to her lips and kissed them. "Absolutely delicious…if you don't mind burning your tonsils out, as Daniel would say."

A nervous titter escaped Ellie's lips, but eating dinner with Arnie—at the ranch or anywhere else— wasn't on her to-do list. Or, more importantly, on Arnie's list, despite what he'd said about Ellie's intelligence and looks. Those words had been for Vanna's benefit, hadn't they?

"It's sweet of you to ask. But you know, I'm still settling in." She gave Mindy another quick hug. "We'll get together soon, I promise." *Sometime when Arnie is far, far away.*

"But you and Arnie used to have a thing going. I thought you'd want to—"

"That *thing* was a long time ago, Mindy." Ellie didn't imagine for a moment that Arnie would want a repeat of their past. "Sometimes you just can't go back."

Waving goodbye to Mindy, Ellie ushered her daughter outside.

A few minutes later, as she pulled into the driveway of her mother's house, she thought about how the tension between her and Arnie—the undercurrent of anger he exuded—was her fault.

In a small town such as this, she would be seeing him often. She needed to clear the air. Apologize. Whether he acknowledged or accepted her apology was up to him.

She needed to make the effort.

Chapter Five

Wiping her sweaty palm unobtrusively on her skirt, Ellie braced herself Thursday evening for whatever might happen at the school board meeting. She kept a smile on her face, desperately trying not to let her nerves show. Whatever happened tonight was important to the future of Ability Counts.

Standing at the back door of the Potter Creek Elementary School multipurpose room, she greeted parents and supporters of Ability Counts as they arrived. She gave each person one of the campaign-style buttons she'd ordered in Manhattan so they could demonstrate the community's support to the school trustees.

They were, after all, elected officials.

"Hello, Mrs. Axelrod," she said, handing Nancy's mother a button. "Thank you for coming tonight."

Mrs. Axelrod pinned the red, white and blue button on the lapel of her lightweight jacket.

Smiling, Ellie turned to greet the next parent coming in the door.

Instead of a parent, however, it was Arnie who wheeled into the multipurpose room, Sheila trotting proudly along beside him. Dressed in a long-sleeved Western-cut shirt with a turquoise bolo tie, Arnie looked every bit the contemporary Indian chief come to take charge. His white shirt set off his sun-burnished complexion, and the squint lines formed a fan at the corners of his eyes.

"Looks like you're the flower girl passing out roses at a wedding," he said.

Her eyes flared at his mentioning a *wedding,* and she struggled to dismiss the comment as meaningless. "As you know, we're hoping for a sea of red, white and blue to influence the board members."

"Hope it works." He patted his chest right over his heart. "Pin away."

She hesitated. Everyone else had pinned on their own button.

Trying for casual, she handed Arnie the box of pins, took one and bent down to pin it on his shirt. Her face close to his, she caught the hint of mint on his breath and the faint aroma of a woodsy aftershave on his smooth cheeks.

Her fingers trembled as she slid the pin through the fabric of his shirt.

"Careful. I bleed easy."

She lifted her gaze from the pin to his eyes. Dark. Deep as a mountain pool. Captivating. They immobilized her with their intensity.

She pricked herself. "Ouch!" Stepping back, she sucked on the tip of her finger, tasting blood.

His lips curved up ever so slightly. "Maybe I ought to pin it on myself."

"Good idea." A tremor shook her voice, and she licked her lips. She handed him the pin, which he attached to his shirt with ease.

"Nothing to it." The amused crook of his brow caused a little flip of Ellie's stomach.

Only when he wheeled down the aisle did Ellie take another breath. That man had the most amazing effect on her, not that it mattered. Obviously, her effect on him was negative, a keep-away-from-me reaction, as though she were the carrier of a dreaded disease.

Except he'd asked her to pin the button on him.

The closest she'd been to him in the past eight years.

A shiver raised gooseflesh on her arms. *Close enough for a kiss.*

The multipurpose room had begun to fill, and the school trustees were beginning to take their places on the risers at the front. Five of the six trustees were men; two of them she recognized as merchants in town. The one woman, who looked to be in her sixties, was wearing an Ability Counts pin. No doubt Vanna's friend and a supporter.

When the chairman gaveled the meeting to order, Vanna signaled Ellie to come sit next to her in the front row. She started forward before she realized she'd have to squeeze past Arnie, whose wheelchair was parked at the end of the row, in order to get to the seat Vanna had indicated.

So be it. Being up front to support the expansion of Ability Counts was part of her job. Her career. Arnie would simply have to live with it.

So would she, Ellie thought as she eased past first Sheila, then Arnie, to take her seat.

"How'd we do for supporters?" Vanna asked.

Ellie showed her the box of pins. She'd started with fifty, and now there were less than ten.

Vanna smiled and gave her a thumbs-up. "Our families are loyal. The trustees have to give us that."

Ellie agreed. But that didn't mean the trustees would vote their way. Based on her research, no school board in the state of Montana had yet approved a charter school, claiming all the limited tax dollars should be used to support public schools. If Vanna could pull this off, it would be amazing.

It didn't take long to get through the agenda to the request from Ability Counts.

"I believe Ms. Coulter wishes to speak to her request," the board president said.

Vanna stood. "I do, Mr. Wright. Thank you." She made her way to the podium.

Ellie remembered having Patrick Wright as her government teacher in high school. Retired now, he'd been an adequate teacher, she supposed, although the subject hadn't been of much interest to her. Now she wished she'd paid more attention.

"Honorable trustees, ladies and gentlemen," Vanna

began. "I'm sure most of you are aware of Ability Counts Preschool and our specialized program to integrate disabled youngsters and mainstream them with 'normal' children. Although, in my view, every child is an individual with unique abilities, so using the term 'normal' is a misnomer. I'm grateful that a good many of our parents and friends are here this evening to support turning Ability Counts into a charter school." She turned to the audience. "Thank you all for coming."

Vanna went on to describe studies that proved the value of early mainstreaming of disabled children, the benefits to the normal students as well and the advantages to the community such a school would provide.

Then she invited Arnie to speak.

He wheeled himself to the podium. Vanna handed him the microphone before she took her seat again with an audible sigh and an expression that suggested she was bone weary.

Ellie gave her employer an encouraging smile.

Arnie addressed the trustees with Sheila sitting alertly at his side, almost as though she was witnessing to the need for special programs for the disabled, as well.

"As most of you know, I became disabled as an adult. I'd already ridden a horse, played football, gone out on dates. But imagine what it's like for a child who spends his entire life with his peers literally looking down on him, running faster, jumping higher than he can. How does he gain his self-esteem when he is so different? Not by shunting him off with others who have the same problems. No, he or she has to be accepted and befriended by those who don't see him or her as different.

"That's what Ability Counts accomplishes by integrating young children in a way that makes them all feel normal."

Ellie's heart expanded with pride in the school's accomplishments and in Arnie's ability to communicate the value of Vanna's dream. She knew the audience didn't see Arnie as disabled. Not in any way that mattered. He was far too competent and confident, a natural leader. A man to be reckoned with.

She wished her mother could see Arnie as she did. Surely she'd realize how lucky any woman would feel to be loved by such a man.

And how stupid Ellie felt for having walked away from even the possibility. At nineteen, she'd been too young to fully realize what she was giving up.

A few parents took a turn at the microphone; then the trustees stated their positions.

The one woman on the board supported Ability Counts. The men, however, cited practicalities: budget limitations, public funds for public schools, adequate existing programs.

The final vote was five to one against creating a charter school.

Dipping her head in disappointment, Ellie closed her eyes and tried to accept the trustees' verdict. In the past few years, she'd learned that God's will didn't always coincide with what she wanted—or thought she wanted.

But in the end she had to trust the Lord knew what He was doing.

That was a leap of faith that didn't always come easily.

Vanna patted her on the shoulder. "Chin up, my dear. This was only the first skirmish. The battle has barely begun. Let's have a cup of coffee and mull over our strategy for the next round."

She smelled of citrus. Oranges ripening in the sun, he thought.

Using the hand controls of his specially equipped van, Arnie drove to the diner after the meeting. He chided himself for letting Ellie get so close. For agreeing to have coffee with her and Vanna. For risking the temptation of being near her again.

What had he been thinking?

He had to be the biggest glutton for punishment this side of the Continental Divide. If he kept this up, it would be all downhill from now on.

"Your master isn't the swiftest wheel on the chair," he said to Sheila, who was safely harnessed on the floor behind him.

Apparently agreeing, Sheila whined and laid her head down on her outstretched paws.

Vanna and Ellie had beaten him into town. Vanna held open the diner's door, and he wheeled inside.

The interior of Potter Creek Diner was decorated in early Western decor with paneled walls, old photos of rodeo cowboys and stuffed animal heads mounted around the room. Although Arnie had done some deer and elk hunting in the days when he'd been able to walk, he'd never been eager to have the animals stuffed and mounted in his house. It was enough that they'd provided meat for the family and neighbors.

"Hey, Ivy." He wheeled his way through the maze of tables to where the owner's daughter had made room at a table for his chair. No other customers were around, and it was only an hour until closing. "Not much action here during the late shift this evening."

"It was busier early." In her early twenties, Ivy had dark eyes and brunet hair, which she wore in a ponytail when she was working. "I don't mind working late. When it's quiet, I can get my homework done."

"College, right?" he asked.

A flash of pride shone in her eyes. "I'm majoring in fine arts, but I've gotta take a whole bunch of art history classes if I want to graduate."

"Good for you," Vanna said, taking the seat opposite him. "Do you know Ellen James? She grew up in town and came back to teach in my preschool. This is Ivy Nelson."

The two younger women greeted each other.

Ellie sat down in the chair next to Arnie. Close enough that he could see the reflection of the overhead lights in her striking blue eyes. He inhaled, wondering if he could catch that citrus scent again, then chided himself for being such a fool.

"What can I get for you folks?" Ivy asked.

"Just coffee for me," Vanna said.

"I'd better have decaf," Ellie said.

Arnie looked up at Ivy. "Make mine the leaded variety, and I'll have a dish of your double dark chocolate ice cream."

"You got it." Ivy headed back behind the counter to round up their order.

An "I remember" smile tilted Ellie's lips. "You and Mindy always were chocoholics."

"Some things never change," he said, his voice low and filled with the same memories.

She glanced away. "And some things do."

An ache bloomed in his chest for what might have been. He forcefully tamped it down. "So, Vanna, what's our next strategy?"

"I didn't really believe the trustees would go for the charter idea, but it was worth a try." She rotated her head as though trying to loosen the tension in her neck. "Their denial means we'll have to fund the expansion from some other source and run Ability Counts as a private school."

"That will be pretty expensive, particularly for families already burdened with medical bills for their children," Ellie commented.

"That's why we need a generous funding source. I don't want to have to turn any child away."

As Ivy delivered their coffees and his ice cream, Arnie considered the difficulty of raising large sums of money both for expansion and ongoing support. The need posed a gigantic hurdle for Ability Counts. More

so than for Paralympics, which was a national organization.

Vanna blew on her coffee before taking a sip. "I had
an architect produce a concept drawing of the expanded
building and grounds. Our next step is to convince the
city council to approve a building permit."

"Do you own the land?" Ellie asked.

"The Ability Counts corporation does. Two years
ago Willie Tompkins donated enough adjacent land for
the buildings and a play yard."

Arnie spooned some ice cream into his mouth and
felt the kick of a sugar high. He knew Tompkins. The
octogenarian was said to be related to the original Caleb
Potter, who founded the town. Vanna must have done
some fancy schmoozing to get the old guy to deed the
land to the school.

"I've already talked to the mayor," Vanna said.
"Arnie, do you know any of the council members personally?"

He shrugged. "I've had some business dealings with
Ted Rojas. He's an okay guy."

"Good. See if you can get an appointment with him."
Vanna turned to Ellie. "Why don't you try to meet with
Jeffrey Robbins? Try to find out where he would stand."

Alarm bells went off in Arnie's head. Jeffrey Robbins was the slickest guy in town, not someone Arnie
wanted Ellie anywhere near. From the stories he'd
heard, Robbins had broken a dozen women's hearts
from here to Bozeman. "Robbins has been involved

with some shaky real estate development deals. Maybe I ought to talk to him."

Ellie's forehead pleated and her brows drew together. "If I only have to find out his position, I think I can manage that."

"Yeah, well, he's sort of a ladies' man. If he gives you a line… Well, don't fall for it." That was a stupid comment, he realized. Knowing it was none of his business who Ellie saw or what line she fell for, he turned his attention back to his ice cream. The rich flavor of chocolate suddenly tasted bitter on his tongue.

"Thanks for the warning, but I think I'll be able to handle it."

A stab of what had to be heartburn caught Arnie in the chest. He shoved his ice cream dish aside. "Sure. No problem."

"Well, you two…" Vanna stood, which caused Sheila to scramble to her feet, as well. "I've had a long day, so I'll be on my way home. Enjoy your coffee." She placed a ten-dollar bill on the table to cover the check. She quickly turned and headed out the door.

Surprised by Vanna's abrupt departure, Arnie said, "Guess I should get back to the ranch. Morning chores come earlier than I would like."

Ellie's hand covered his on the table. "Don't go just yet. I think we need to talk."

He looked at her hand, her fair skin almost white against his darker complexion. Her fingers delicate compared to his work-roughened hands, all nicks and scratches. Her nails short and neatly trimmed. Her palm like a soft, cool caress on his skin.

His throat tightened and he withdrew his hand. "What's to talk about?"

"I owe you an apology for how I handled things after your accident."

"A wise man once said an apology was about as valuable as an empty bowl of sugar."

She visibly flinched, and Arnie chastised himself for being so rough on her. She was trying to do the right thing. What had happened to his ability to forgive and forget?

"I'm sorry." Her voice was low and filled with regret. Her eyes focused solely on his, darkening in their intensity. "There's no excuse for what I did. I was young and frightened. Those first few days you were in the hospital, I'd never seen you so helpless. When you told me to go away, I panicked."

He straightened and lifted his jaw, his defenses on alert. "I never said any such thing." He wouldn't have, couldn't have, told her to go away.

"You were in and out of consciousness for days. How do you know what you said or didn't say?"

Whatever happened he couldn't sit there watching her pain thin her lips and wrinkle her forehead and tears glitter in her eyes. He was a coward when it came to Ellie. Too chickenhearted to take a gamble and lose.

Shaking his head, he rolled back from the table. "Forget about it, Ellie. It's ancient history. Nothing has changed. I'm exactly what you were afraid I'd become.

I've got a handicapped license plate on my van to prove it."

Not wanting to hear what she might say, he charged toward the door, pressing hard. The thought that she might agree was too painful to contemplate. Too painful to risk hearing the words from the woman he had once loved.

The woman who had left him when he needed her the most.

When he'd worked his way behind the wheel of the van, he glanced toward the diner. Ellie was standing in the doorway, her hand covering her mouth.

Guilt nailed him in the sternum, driving the air from his lungs.

I'm sorry. How much courage it must have taken for her to speak those two simple words.

How much more courage would he need to accept them?

Chapter Six

The pain started in Ellie's chest, radiating outward until it throbbed at her temples. Her throat was so constricted, she could barely breathe. A tremor had shaken her body as she watched Arnie storm out the diner.

Fighting tears, she'd followed him as far as the door. Saw him get in his van. A minute later, the van's headlights shattered the darkness and spotlighted Ellie.

Spotlighted her failings.

Dear God, how could I have hurt Arnie so badly? How can I make it right again?

She rubbed her temple with her fingertips. He hadn't accepted her apology. From the way he acted, he never would.

Guilt was the hammer that pummeled her conscience, made her blood pulse icy cold through her veins and blurred her vision. *I'm so sorry.*

The last day she'd seen Arnie in the hospital, he had made it abundantly clear she should leave him alone. A part of her had not wanted to believe him. She could be stubborn. Wait it out until his injuries had healed. By then he would change his mind, she'd hoped.

Then he'd rolled over, turning his back on her, and she'd lost hope. Her foolish pride had demanded that she do just as he'd said. She'd leave him alone.

Exactly as her mother had encouraged her to do.

Now she knew she'd been wrong. Lacking in trust that she and Arnie, together, could have made a go of it.

Now it was too late.

With a discouraged sigh, she drove home. She found her mother in the small living room with its aging, overstuffed furniture, watching a police story on TV.

"How did the school board meeting go?"

"They turned down our request." Beaten and dejected, Ellie shrugged out of her lightweight jacket and draped it across the back of the couch. "Did Torie get to bed on time?"

"Oh, yes. We read a book together. She really is reading, you know. And here she isn't even five yet. Of course, you were an early reader, too. I remember when you were four, the librarian was so impressed with you."

"I remember. Sorry, but I'm really tired. Thanks for watching Torie, Mom. I'm going to bed. See you in the morning."

Ellie fled to the bedroom that had been hers growing up. The twin bed with a trundle for company, the spread navy-blue with red-and-white squares. Posters of punk rock and heavy metal musical groups she had once favored had been removed, but the marks left by masking tape were still visible. She needed to repaint the room, make it a reflection of who she was now, not the impulsive girl of her youth.

She sat down heavily on the side of the bed.

Tears blurred her vision as she opened the drawer in the bed table and retrieved her Bible. The faux leather cover was worn from repeated use over the past five years, the gold lettering flaked away.

She laid the Bible in her lap. It opened automatically to the passage she had long ago committed to memory: Proverbs 3:5 Trust in the Lord with all your heart and lean not on your own understanding.

All Ellie could do was to lead as Christian a life as she was able and ask for forgiveness when she fell short.

That ethereal goal had never been harder than it was tonight.

She couldn't change the past. But how could she make the future right?

"Will I get to ride Patches again?" Torie asked from the back of the school van.

It was Friday morning, and the preschoolers were on their way to the O'Brien ranch for their weekly riding lesson. A knot of dread tightened in Ellie's stomach at the thought of seeing Arnie after the way things had been left last night.

"I don't know, honey," she said.

"I hope I get to go fast this time. I don't like a poky horse."

Torie received a chorus of agreement from her classmates.

"Just remember you all have to do what Daniel and Arnie tell you to do. We want you to be safe."

Ellie's heart accelerated as the van bumped over the cattle guard at the entrance to the ranch. A few head of beef cattle grazed near the roadway. They looked up, slowly chewing their cud. Ellie sincerely wished she could be that calm.

She inhaled a bracing breath. She'd done what she could to make amends. If that wasn't enough to restore a bit of the friendship she'd once shared with Arnie, she'd have to let it go. Let God handle it. If He didn't think she deserved to be friends with Arnie, then she'd have to live with that knowledge.

As she parked, she noticed plywood now covered the framing on the house under construction and a river-stone chimney had been erected. Cutouts in the plywood showed where the windows would be. Progress was definitely being made.

"All right, we're here," Ellie said.

The children cheered and scrambled for the exits.

"Go join Miss Vanna and her class."

Keeping an eye out for Arnie, Ellie trailed along behind her students. By the time she reached Vanna, Daniel had appeared out of the barn, his young helper right behind him.

"Good morning, kids. You ready to ride?"

"Yes!" they responded in a shrill chorus.

"Great!" He grinned broadly. "Let's start with Miss Vanna's group. You go with Marc. He'll help you mount up. The rest of you can come with me."

"Where's Arnie?" Torie asked.

"He had some business in Bozeman this morning."

Relief and disappointment battled for primacy, the former easing the tension in Ellie's neck and shoulders, the latter dropping like a rock to her stomach.

Was he avoiding her? Or did he really have business elsewhere? She didn't know and tried not to care.

Daniel led her flock of children into the barn. "You all remember where we keep the brushes?"

Nancy, on her crutches, led the race to the Peg-Board where brushes, hoof picks and other grooming tools were hung in place.

Ellie experienced a moment of pride at the independent streak Nancy was beginning to exhibit.

Gathering the children around a placid buckskin mare named Marigold, Daniel put the children to work combing her mane and brushing her coat. Ellie steadied the step stool Billy was using to reach the horse's mane.

"Sorry to hear the school board turned down the charter request," Daniel said, standing next to Ellie, where they could both keep track of the children.

"Evidently Vanna expected they would. She's starting to look for private funding."

He eased a child away from the back of the mare. "Don't get so close. She can kick you," he warned.

The child made a wide pass around Marigold's rump so he could work on the other side.

"Mindy asked me to invite you, Torie and your mother to Sunday supper after church," Daniel said.

Ellie's head snapped around. "This Sunday?"

"Sure. Assuming you don't have other plans."

"Um, no, but—"

"Mommy," Torie whispered. "If we come to supper, maybe Arnie will let me ride a horse again."

Amazing what little ears can hear. "We'll talk about that later, honey." Ellie stepped back away from Torie and her classmates. "I'm not sure us coming to dinner is a good idea," she whispered to Daniel.

His dark eyes widened, raising his brows. "Why not?"

She puffed out a weary sigh. "Arnie is still angry with me for leaving town after his accident."

"After all this time? I know you two were once an item, but I thought he'd gotten past you leaving town and all."

"I'm afraid not. I've tried to apologize, but he wasn't interested in hearing it."

Taking off his Stetson, Daniel ran his fingers through his raven-black hair before resettling his hat. "It's not like him to hold a grudge."

"It's not a grudge, exactly." Far more personal than that, she suspected. More like a deep wound that refused to heal.

Carson wheeled up to Daniel. "I'm done brushing the parts I can reach. Can I feed Marigold an apple now?"

"Sure." He fetched a plastic baggie of cut-up apples from a nearby workbench. "Okay, kids. Put away your brushes, and you can give Marigold a treat. Remember, one at a time."

The children delighted in the graze of Marigold's soft lips on their palms as she delicately plucked a quartered apple from their hands.

By the time each child had a turn feeding Marigold, it was time to switch with the children who had been riding.

"I look at it this way," Daniel said to Ellie before she went out to the corral. "Mindy's your friend. She's invited you to have dinner with us on Sunday. Arnie's invited, too. If he doesn't want to come, that's his choice."

Ellie wished the decision was that simple. She didn't want to compound Arnie's bad feelings toward her or hurt him all over again. But she did want to renew her friendship with Mindy. Daniel, too.

She had no idea how her mother would react to the invitation.

"Let me think about it. Tell Mindy I'll give her a call or stop by the knit shop."

As soon as Ellie and her daughter returned home that afternoon, Torie went running into the house to find her grandma BarBar. Ellie followed her inside.

"I got to ride Patches again, and the boy let me steer by myself, but he didn't want me to go fast."

A warm smile creased Barbara's face. "That's nice, dear."

"And, Grandma." Torie bopped around from one foot to another like a Mexican jumping bean. "Mr. Daniel invited us to dinner on Sunday, and maybe I can ride on the horsey again. Can't I, Mommy?"

Ellie cringed inwardly. She'd planned to approach the dinner invitation when she and her mother were alone.

"I'm not sure we're going to accept the invitation, honey."

"But, Mommy, I want to ride Patches again!" She planted her fists on her hips like an angry fishwife and glared at Ellie.

"We'll talk about it later," Ellie insisted.

"I want to talk about it now!"

Controlling her own temper and her roiling emotions regarding Arnie, Ellie forced patience into her voice. "I don't want to give you a time-out, Victoria. You know you're not allowed to talk to me like that."

"But, Mommy…"

Ellie held up one finger as a warning.

Her daughter's face crumbled into a despairing expression, and tears bubbled to the surface.

When Ellie held up a second finger, Torie sobbed aloud, whirled and ran to her bedroom, slamming the door behind her. Given that show of temper, Ellie could only imagine what fun having a teenager in the house would be.

"You're going to dinner at the O'Brien ranch?" her mother asked.

"We've all been invited. I was going to discuss it with you later."

"Is he going to be there?"

"If you mean Arnie, I don't know if he'll be there or not. The invitation was extended by Daniel on Mindy's behalf and includes you."

Her hand shaking slightly, Barbara picked up a pair of Torie's jeans that she'd been mending. "I can't think of any reason they'd invite me."

"Mindy stayed at our house a couple of nights that summer when she visited Aunt Martha. I'm sure she doesn't want you to feel left out."

"Well, I don't want to interfere with you young people. You'll enjoy yourselves more without an old lady around to cramp your fun."

Ellie exhaled a weary sigh. "Mother, I wish you'd get to know Arnie better. He isn't nearly as incapacitated as Uncle Bob was. Yes, he has some limitations, but he's every inch the man Dad was." Smart. Good with children. Except for his paralysis, physically the equal of any man. And heart-stoppingly handsome.

Barbara's face turned red, and Ellie knew she'd gone too far. Her and her quick retorts. When would she ever grow up?

"I'm sorry, Mother. I didn't mean to—"

"It's no matter. You go if you must, but give Mindy my regrets. I'll manage Sunday supper on my own."

The larger question was, how would Ellie manage sitting at the same table with Arnie without making a fool of herself?

* * *

A warm breeze swept in through the window openings of Arnie's unfinished house Saturday afternoon and blew the roll of blueprints off the worktable.

"Sheila, pick up," he commanded.

He needn't have bothered. Sheila had moved almost before the blueprints hit the floor, retrieving them for Arnie.

"Good girl." He nuzzled his face against hers and scratched behind her ears. She was an extension of his arms, a substitute for his legs, and made his life easier in a thousand little ways. Getting a service dog was an admission of his limitations and one of the smartest things he'd ever done.

A load of drywall had been delivered that afternoon and was stacked in the corner. Arnie would start putting it up this coming week, when he had some free time.

Pride drove him to be a part of the construction of his own house. He couldn't climb a ladder or install shingles on the roof. But what was between the floor and as high as his arms could reach would be his own doing.

After a day filled with the sound of his buddies installing siding and insulation and making smart remarks, the house was quiet now. Peaceful. On the breeze, the occasional birdsong or quiet low of his cattle reached him, the nicker of Daniel's quarter horses and the buzz of flies nearer at hand. There'd been a time when he hadn't thought he'd live to hear the sounds of the ranch again.

The moment he realized Daniel had lost control of his truck. The sight of the boulder filling the windshield just before they crashed.

The excruciating pain that followed.

And then the darkness that had cocooned him. He hadn't wanted to leave that darkness. There was safety there. A kind of peace.

But they brought him back, the doctors and nurses. Daniel. And Ellie, holding his hand every time he broke through the surface of that black, bottomless hole.

Tears burned in his eyes, and he swiped them away with the back of his hand.

Sheila whined.

"It's okay, girl. It's okay."

At the sound of approaching footsteps, Arnie shook off his morose mood.

"Hey, bro, Mindy says dinner's ready in ten minutes."

He wheeled toward Daniel. "Be right with you. Gotta clean up first."

"No problem." Daniel stepped out of his way. "Ellie called a few minutes ago. Mindy invited her and Torie to Sunday supper. She accepted."

Arnie braked his wheelchair hard. "She's coming to dinner? Tomorrow?"

"Yep. After church. Her mother was invited, too, but she declined."

Anger pounded against his ribs like a four-pound hammer. "So what am I supposed to do?"

"Come to supper, like you always do. Mindy's slow cooking a roast. All you have to do is show up."

Show up and face the one thing he could never dare dream of having—Ellie.

"I'll eat at the diner tomorrow." He gave the wheelchair a shove. His chair didn't budge.

"What's with you, man? You can't go on avoiding Ellie. It's not like she was the one who put you in that chair. I did that."

A muscle flexed in his jaw. "Let go of my chair."

"She's the best thing that could happen to you. You've been wearing your heart on your sleeve since she showed up. Give it a chance, bro."

Whipping his chair around hard, Arnie broke Daniel's grip and wheeled away from him. "I'll decide what's good for me, Danny boy. Not you. Not Mindy." And not Vanna Coulter, who, he suspected, had matchmaking on her mind, too. "Stay out of it, all of you."

He would not be coerced or cajoled into playing gracious host to Ellie and her daughter. And he wouldn't be suckered by well-meaning matchmakers into courting her, either.

That was not how it was going to be.

Chapter Seven

Upset with himself, Arnie knew his conscience, and maybe his good sense and sleepless night, had gotten to him. He decided not to eat Sunday supper at the diner. He couldn't be that rude to Ellie and her daughter. It wasn't their fault he was no longer the man he used to be.

He'd seen Ellie at church this morning. She'd had a bright, friendly smile for everyone she greeted. Her shiny auburn hair swung loosely at her shoulders as she walked, catching the sunlight like warm flames, and stirring thoughts he didn't want to entertain.

Didn't dare entertain.

Because the truth was, he wanted to touch her hair, lace the silken strands through his fingers, inhale the citrus scent. Coward that he was, he knew the flames caught in her hair would burn him.

He changed into jeans and a work shirt after he got home from church, and maybe took a little extra time combing his hair. He'd excuse himself as soon as the meal was over, retreat to his house and start putting up the drywall. No harm done.

"You need any help with supper?" he asked Mindy as he rolled into the kitchen, Sheila trotting beside him. The room smelled of beef cooking and freshly baked bread.

"No, I'm good. Thanks." She wore a butcher-style apron printed with colorful quarter horses over her church clothes, which didn't quite hide the growing paunch of her pregnant tummy. "I'll just pour the iced tea and milk and serve everything once Ellie and Torie get here."

"Okay. Let me know if you need me." He wheeled into the living room, where Daniel was sprawled on the couch, reading the Sunday paper.

Glancing out the front window, Arnie spotted Ellie's compact coming up the drive. The dust that rose behind it hung like a brown banner in the still afternoon air.

He swallowed hard and licked his lips. His fingers tapped a syncopated rhythm on the arm of his wheelchair. Maybe he should've gone to the diner, after all.

He beat a retreat to the kitchen. "Ellie's coming down the driveway. I'll pour the iced tea for you."

Mindy whirled and leveled a frown at him. "Why don't you go open the door for her instead?"

"Daniel's in the living room. He'll let her in."

Shaking her head, Mindy tugged off her apron and tossed it over the back of a chair. "Men! Humph! I'll do it."

Temporarily rescued from another face-to-face meeting with Ellie, Arnie blew out a sigh. *Coward!*

The house suddenly filled with girlish laughter, as though Mindy and Ellie were teenagers again. The sound took Arnie back to lazy days spent at the river park, water fights and strolls along the trail on moonlit nights.

He squeezed his eyes shut, but the memories couldn't be easily vanquished.

"Come on into the kitchen," Mindy said. "Everything is ready to go."

"Oh, I love your hardwood floors." Wide-eyed and smiling, Ellie walked into the kitchen. She'd changed into slacks and a sleeveless T-shirt that bared her tanned, slightly freckled arms. "And look at this. Talk about top-of-the-line appliances and miles of counter space. My apartment in Spokane was so small, the whole thing would have fit inside your kitchen."

"Daniel and Arnie did most of the remodeling themselves. They didn't think they needed a formal dining room, so they created a family kitchen."

Ellie came to a halt near the table. "Hello, Arnie."

"Hi." *Great conversation opener,* he admonished himself, not proud that he had turned tongue-tied.

Torie pushed her way past her mother. "Can I sit next to Arnie and his doggy, Mommy? Can I?"

"You'll have to ask Mindy. She's our hostess."

The child looked up at Mindy with her innocent green eyes, her expression angelic, her request impossible to deny.

"Of course you may, sweetie." Mindy handed two glasses of iced tea to Daniel, who put them on the table, then poured two more and a glass of milk for Torie.

Torie plopped down on her knees and started to pet Sheila. "She's such a pretty doggy. Will she ever have babies? Maybe my mommy would let me have one of Sheila's puppies."

Arnie heard Ellie make a choking sound, and he swallowed a laugh. "I'm afraid not, squirt. No puppies for Sheila."

"That's too bad. I think Sheila would make a very, very good mommy."

Daniel carried the roast on a serving platter to the table. "Okay, gang, take a seat and let's eat. I'm starved."

Torie hopped into a chair next to Arnie's place.

"I have to warn you, Ellie." Mindy delivered serving bowls heaped with potatoes and vegetables. "These two cowboys eat enough at one seating to feed the whole population of Haiti." She took her place next to her husband, leaving the other chair next to Arnie vacant.

"Torie may need help cutting up her meat," Ellie said. "If you'd like to scoot over, I can—"

"I think I can handle it." His voice gruffer than he'd intended, Arnie sounded like he had a frog in his throat. Or a chip on his shoulder. "It's okay," he said more gently.

They all held hands while Arnie said grace. He wasn't sure what words he spoke, aware only of Ellie's slender fingers enclosed by his on one side and Torie's small, trusting hand in the other.

Beads of perspiration formed on his forehead and dampened his palms. This could have been his.

His stomach knotted. *Don't think about that.*

Conversation flowed around him as they ate. Talk of the kids they'd known years ago. How much Ellie enjoyed teaching. The success of Knitting and Notions. How well Daniel's breeding program was going for his quarter horses.

Arnie didn't participate much, only answering questions when he was asked.

When they were almost finished eating, he glanced at Torie and caught her slipping Sheila a bite of carrots.

"Oh, oh," he said quietly. "Somebody doesn't like carrots?"

"Sheila likes 'em."

"Maybe so, but it's not good to feed her at the table. She has her own food."

Torie's lower lip puffed out. "It was only one bite."

He winked at her. "No more, okay?"

Her defeated sigh would have blown out a hundred candles on the biggest birthday cake in Potter Creek.

After dinner, Mindy took Ellie and Torie upstairs to see the nursery, a work in progress. Daniel and Arnie cleared the table and put the dishes in the dishwasher.

With that accomplished, Arnie slipped out of the house and wheeled over to his place. He wasn't hiding out, exactly. He simply wanted to get started on the drywall.

With his tool belt hanging on the back of his wheelchair, he hefted a sheet of drywall and rolled to the corner of the living room where he planned to start. Sitting sideways, he settled the sheet into place over the insulation and held it there while he drove in the first nail. It went easily through the gypsum plaster and into the stud with a satisfying thud.

My house, my work.

Backing up, he set more nails in place to hold the board in place. That accomplished, he retrieved another sheet and repeated the process.

When he reached the window opening that looked out over the pasture, he used a straight edge and a utility knife to cut the board to fit.

"Whatcha doing?"

Torie's question startled him, and he nearly stabbed himself with the knife.

He glanced over his shoulder. "I'm putting up drywall so the house will stay nice and warm in the winter."

"Can I help you?"

"I don't think so, squirt."

She squatted down next to Sheila, petting her. "I got bored looking at the baby's room. One time I asked Mommy for a little brother or sister, but she said she couldn't make a baby all by herself. She needs a daddy to help her make one."

Struggling to keep a straight face, Arnie said, "That's right."

She sat cross-legged on the bare floor, and Sheila put her head in Torie's lap. "How come you don't have any childrens? You'd make a good daddy. My daddy didn't want to stay with us, but it's okay. Mommy and me have each other."

He wheeled across the room for another sheet of gypsum wallboard. Torie's conversation was touching on a sore subject. Arnie didn't think he was up for that.

Carrying the board, he wheeled back to the spot where he'd been working. "You're lucky to have your mom. She's a nice lady."

Ellie stepped into the house at just that moment. Her breath caught when she heard his compliment.

"I hope I'm not interrupting," she said, not wanting Arnie to think she'd been eavesdropping.

His head snapped up. She saw him swallow hard, and color raced up his neck to his cheeks.

"Mommy, we were talking about babies."

Ellie's blush rose hotter than Arnie's. He turned away, and she knew it was to hide his laughter.

"Victoria! I…" she sputtered. "I came to tell you Daniel will take you riding on Patches if you'd like."

Like a clown in a music box, Torie popped to her feet, dislodging Sheila, who scrambled out of the child's way.

"Oh, Mommy, I looove to ride Patches. Come see me."

"I will in a minute. Go find Daniel in the corral. He's saddling your horse."

When Torie was out of sight, Ellie said, "I apologize for Torie. I'm afraid she's a bit outspoken."

"She's a real pistol, all right." He lifted his shoulders in what was surely meant to be an easy shrug but looked as stiff as a cardboard cowboy. "No harm, no foul."

Hesitating, she crossed her arms in front of her chest. "Your house is going to be lovely. Lots of open space."

"Easier for me to get around in the wheelchair."

"Of course." She shifted her weight from one foot to the other and glanced outside.

Her curiosity riding high, she didn't want to leave just yet. She wanted to see what his new home looked like, wanted to be able to picture him here in his own place.

"I decided to go for three bedrooms and turn one into my office," he said. "Don't know what I'll do with the third. Probably just pile my extra junk in there."

She knew exactly what she'd do with that extra room. "It's smart to build bigger than you think you'll need. My dad was always adding on rooms or another porch. The house is like a jigsaw puzzle with too many pieces that don't quite fit."

"Do you want a tour?"

Her heart stuttered an extra beat. "I, um, sure."

"Okay." He leaned the gypsum sheet against the wall. "Obviously, this is the living room. That'll be the kitchen." He rolled across the room. "There'll be a breakfast bar here sort of separating the two areas and a view of the mountains out the window over the sink. And down this way are the bedrooms."

She followed him down the hallway, picturing the

furniture that would fill the rooms—leather couches with bright throw pillows in the living room, an oak table in the kitchen that would expand to seat a dozen guests. Walls the color of sandstone with family photographs mounted on them. A family history built step-by-step.

"The master suite is pretty big. There'll be a Jacuzzi in the bathroom, plus a big roll-in shower with a bunch of showerheads." He paused at the bedroom doorway. "Across the hall is what I'll use as my office. Between it and the other bedroom is another bathroom with standard equipment."

"Very nice. I'm sure you'll be happy having your own space."

Wheeling around, he looked up at her. In the interior shadows, his eyes seemed darker than ever. They held a haunted look she couldn't translate. Of wanting? Of need? For her? She couldn't be sure.

"I, um, shouldn't keep you from your work any longer." Her fingers trembling, she touched the silver necklace around her neck. "I'd better rescue Daniel before Torie drives him crazy with questions."

"She does ask some real doozies."

"Yes, she does. Sorry about that." Her face still flushed, she backed up a few steps. "Between horses and doggies and babies, she seems determined to embarrass you with her questions."

"I don't mind. I like kids."

She smiled. "It shows." They'd never gotten as far as talking about the children they might have. She doubted that Arnie had considered the idea, while she… The possibility had more than crossed her mind. For fear of scaring Arnie off, she'd never mentioned their making a family together.

Too late now, she realized with a renewed pang of regret.

"As I said, I'd better go check on Torie." Her heart heavy, she backed out the door.

Minutes later, Arnie saw Ellie emerge from the barn. Daniel had saddled her a horse, and the three of them rode out of the corral, Daniel leading Patches, Torie sitting proudly in the saddle. Ellie laughing as she tried to rein her mount out the gate.

Regret washed over Arnie for the things he couldn't do. Like take Ellie and Torie for a horseback ride out to the creek that ran through the ranch. Or even saddle a horse for her or Torie.

Frustration burned in his gut.

He yanked the tool belt off of his wheelchair and slammed it across the room, where it banged against the wall. He had to get out of here. Not dwell on what couldn't be. He needed the wind in his face to blow away the cobwebs of regret.

He rolled out of his house and into the barn, where he kept his specially equipped ATV. Using the lift bar Daniel had jerry-rigged for him, Arnie levered himself into the seat. Sheila jumped into the back right behind him.

He punched the starter on the ATV, twisted the hand accelerator and rocketed out the open barn door.

His only doubt was that he might not be able to go far enough or fast enough to forget.

Ellie hadn't ridden a horse in eight years. She'd forgotten the feel of her thighs stretching across the saddle, the rhythmic movement of the horse beneath her, the sense of freedom riding a horse gave her.

Later she'd likely remember in detail the penalty for not having ridden in a long time—lots of aches and pains. She was already looking forward to a good soak in a hot bath.

They rode three abreast, Torie in the middle, jabbering about horses, the crows that rose cawing from a stand of pine trees and anything else that flitted through her mind.

Torie's constant chatter didn't seem to bother Daniel, for which Ellie was grateful since her own thoughts remained with Arnie. Wondering if he'd returned to his drywall task. If he was thinking of her.

She eased her mount around to the other side of Daniel so they could talk. "You and your brother seem to get along better now than you did eight years ago," Ellie commented.

"I nearly killed him in that accident. I figure I owe him big-time."

"Does he resent what happened to him?"

"Most days he's okay with what happened. Figures God has some sort of a plan."

Ellie thought that was very generous of Arnie, more so than she might have been under similar circumstances.

"Lately, since Mindy and I got married, I think Arnie's feeling left out," Daniel said.

"Is that why he's building his own house?"

"Yeah. Mindy and I didn't want him to move out. The main house is his, too. But he insisted."

Perhaps Arnie felt more resentment than he wanted to let on. Or perhaps he was planning ahead for his own future.

She licked her slightly dry lips and asked the question that she'd been afraid to raise. "Has Arnie been seeing anyone?"

"You mean a girlfriend? He hasn't dated since the accident. Frankly…" He glanced toward Torie, who seemed to be fully engaged in a discussion with Patches about not stepping on any snakes in the grass. "I think he'd be a lot happier if he found himself a woman and married her."

Apparently not as engaged in her conversation with Patches as Ellie had thought, Torie perked up at Daniel's comment. "When I grow up, I could marry Arnie, and you and Mommy and Mindy and Sheila could come to the wedding."

Daniel covered his bark of laughter with a cough. "I think we ought to leave that up to Arnie, okay?"

For a moment, Ellie couldn't breathe, as though all the air had been sucked out of Montana and replaced with hope.

Hope that Arnie would find happiness with a woman.
Hope that she would be that woman.
And fear that she wouldn't be.

Chapter Eight

By the middle of the week there was a hint of autumn in the air and the poplars near her mother's old barn were brushed with a touch of gold. This was Ellie's favorite time of year, except her nerves were on edge and she hadn't been sleeping well.

She hadn't seen Arnie since Sunday, but the memory of the horseback ride and Daniel's comments about his brother had stuck in her head as if they'd been glued to her brain.

It's none of your business, Ellen James. Get it out of your head right now!

Ellie had arranged to meet city councilman Jeffrey Robbins at city hall to talk about permits to expand Ability Counts and get his support, if possible. A one-story brick building shared with the police department, city hall was easy to navigate and Ellie had no difficulty finding Councilman Robbins's office.

From the moment he greeted her, Ellie developed an

uncomfortable feeling about the councilman. Her instincts told her Arnie was right. She didn't want anything to do with this smooth talker.

He seated her in one of the two guest chairs in front of his impressive desk and sat down beside her. Leaning away from him, Ellie told him about the plans for the school and gave him the printed materials she'd brought with her. He placed those on his desk without even glancing at them.

"I've heard something about her plans," he said. "You'll be requesting a building permit, I imagine."

"Yes, Ms. Coulter is putting the request together. I've been asked to get a sense of where you might stand on the permit."

"I didn't see the request on the agenda for next week."

"I think Vanna is working out some of the specifics before she brings the package before the city council."

"Ah, good. Then we'll have some time to get acquainted." He slid his arm along the back of her chair. "It will take me a day or two to read your material. Why don't we get together Friday to discuss it, say, for dinner? There's a nice little place I know—"

Ellie stood. "No, thank you, Mr. Robbins. I'm sure if you call Ms. Coulter, she can answer your questions."

His expression darkened, and she could tell he wasn't used to being rejected by a woman. Personally, she'd pick a rattlesnake for a date before she'd go out with him. "Thank you for your time, Mr. Robbins."

Her head held high, she marched out of his office.

"You may be sorry, Ms. James," he called after her.

"Not in this lifetime," she mumbled under her breath.

Arnie had been only partially right about Robbins. He might think of himself as a ladies' man, but any woman who fell for his phony lines should go back to Dating 101. She knew enough to stay clear of a guy whose ego was bigger than the Titanic, because sure as the sun comes up in the morning, he'd sink to the bottom from the weight of all that false pride.

Ellie had learned that the hard way—from Torie's father, Jake Radigan. Smooth as silk and slippery as winter ice when it came to commitment.

By the time she gave birth to Torie, Ellie realized Jake's hasty departure had been the Lord's way of teaching her a lesson and giving her a blessing she'd never forget.

She drove back to the school to report on her meeting and lack of success with Robbins.

Sitting in her employer's office a few minutes later, she told Vanna about the meeting. "I'm really sorry. I think I blew it. In fact, Robbins might vote against the project out of spite because I refused his advances."

Sniffing in disdain, Vanna shook her head. "I knew he was full of himself, but I didn't know Jeffrey was a sleazy character, too. I'm glad you put him firmly in his place."

"Which may be firmly against the expansion," Ellie warned.

"There are seven members of the town council, including the mayor, who has been a personal friend of mine for years." She gazed out her office window toward the play yard, where extended-day-care children were engaged in trying to climb a thick rope hanging from a sprawling oak tree. "With any luck, I think we can count on at least four votes."

"Unless he can persuade others to vote against us."

"I think we'll start a letter-writing campaign," Vanna said, still watching the children outside. "If we get enough support from the townspeople, the council will have to listen to them. Democracy at work, as they say."

"Do you think a few letters will be enough to sway the council members?"

Vanna turned back to Ellie with a resolute smile. "You've got to have faith, child. That's what has kept me going all these years. I'm not ready to quit just yet, the Lord willing."

Something ominous in Vanna's tone, like a flat bass note on a piano, sent chills down Ellie's spine.

Vanna's expression hadn't changed, her determined smile still in place. Even so, Ellie felt a pain so sharp, she feared it was a harbinger of the future. And prayed it was only her imagination.

A group of Paralympic athletes had taken to training at a Bozeman high school track during evening hours. The school's coach had arranged for lights and the use of the shower facilities.

"Come on, O'Brien. God gave you two good arms. Use 'em." Carrying a stopwatch in his hand, Coach

Milton ran along inside the track, on the grass, badgering Arnie, cutting the corners to keep up with him. "You're wheeling that thing like a girl. Dig, man, dig."

Despite the cool air, sweat ran down Arnie's face and pooled under his arms. It felt like he was back on the Potter Creek football team, only the workouts were ten times as rugged. He dug into the wheels so hard, the friction burned through his gloves and his lungs labored for air. He'd gone nearly forty laps, ten miles, around the track, and all of it at full throttle.

"You got ten days, O'Brien. Ten days until that Thompson character from Billings is gonna try to whup you good."

Not this time, Arnie thought as he rocketed around the final turn. Thompson would eat his dust.

A man in his fifties, the coach wore a school sweatshirt and running shorts that revealed his prosthetic left leg, the result of a motorcycle accident. "This is where you sprint, O'Brien. Don't let up now. It's the final hundred yards. Dig, man, dig. He's gonna catch you."

From somewhere, Arnie found one more ounce of strength he hadn't yet used. He poured it on, pushing hard past the finish line. Only then did he lean back and coast, drawing in great gulps of air to fill his overtaxed lungs.

The coach jogged after him. He held the stopwatch to show Arnie his finishing time.

Totally spent, Arnie managed a weak smile. "My personal best."

"You did it, son." He slapped Arnie on the back.

"This weekend you'll have to make the same time on a hilly course and keep it up for twenty-six miles."

Arnie groaned. The coach was a lunatic. He never let up, never let anybody say "I quit." His high school athletes had to hate him, but they kept coming back year after year. Because they kept winning.

Arnie planned to do the same. Right after he bought a couple more pairs of gloves.

"I've been thinking about our letter-writing campaign," Ellie said. She'd arrived at school early and gone directly to Vanna's office. All night her head had been spinning with ideas, and she'd gotten little sleep. "I thought we'd have our best impact by having our children draw pictures of the school that we'll build, and each picture would be signed by the student. We can put those in a thick folder. With any luck, the pictures will be so touching, council members won't be able to tell our little darlings no to expanding the school.

"Then we have to encourage our parents to write actual letters." She handed Vanna the sample letter she'd composed that morning, along with a memo to parents. "And finally, we need to reach out to the community to write letters, too. I made up a flyer to distribute around town. I thought I'd ask the pastor at church to say something from the pulpit, too."

Leaning back in her desk chair, Vanna scanned the letter and flyer, nodding as she read.

"Young lady, you've been holding out on me. You're

a born politician, and I mean that in the most complimentary way."

Laughing, Ellie shook her head. "Politics hold no interest for me. But I do want to see the school built. That's why I jumped at the chance to join your staff and move back to Potter Creek."

"You may not want to get involved in politics, per se, but you have the political instincts necessary to run a successful nonprofit organization. And believe me, a lot of politicking is necessary when you're the director of a school like this."

"Which is exactly why I'm content to teach the children and let you do the politicking."

Cocking her head, Vanna eyed Ellie in a way that unsettled her. "We'll see, my dear. We'll see." Standing, Vanna said, "You talk to the teachers about having the children draw pictures for us. I'll make copies of the letter to send home with the children this afternoon, and I'll do up some flyers to post around town."

"We could get something in the newspaper, too."

"Excellent idea. I'll put you in charge of talking to Amy Thurgood at the *Potter Creek Courier*. Give her copies of the material you gave Councilman Robbins. Maybe Amy will write up a story for us."

The rest of the morning sped by. Ellie's class of four-year-olds decided they wanted lots of swings and slides at the new school, a vegetable garden, plenty of books to read and a piano. On top of the school building they wanted to see an American flag flying.

Individually, they used crayons to create a picture of the school of their dreams, then added their name in their childish handwriting. Each artistic effort carried a powerful message no adult could match—or deny.

During the lunch period, Ellie met with the other teachers in the conference room. She showed them the pictures her students had drawn.

"I think if you let your students have free rein with their ideas, I'm confident they'll come up with some very touching arguments in favor of Ability Counts."

Dawn pulled the folder closer. "These are really great. Was this your idea?"

"Vanna wanted something that would persuade the council members," Ellie said. "Kids seem to know instinctively what buttons to push."

Peggy laughed out loud. "Don't you know, when my own two darlings were young, they could wrap anyone around their little fingers without half trying."

Torie was pretty good at that game, too, Ellie acknowledged. Not only with her, but with Arnie, as well. It seemed her daughter could turn Arnie to mush with the crook of a baby finger. Regretfully, Ellie didn't have the same power over him.

With her fellow teachers briefed, Ellie left Torie in extended day care during the afternoon. She went into town, to the newspaper office, located on Main Street in a one-story stucco building with wooden siding. The headline on the most recent edition of the newspaper, which was posted in the front window, announced School Board Approves Principal's Contract.

Given that world news mainly involved wars, floods and general mayhem, Ellie decided Potter Creek was as close to perfect as she could get here on earth.

A cowbell clanked as she opened the door, and she caught a whiff of printer's ink and old newspapers. After a single step inside, she halted abruptly, freezing in place. Her heart ping-ponged around in her chest, and her face flushed, as though she'd spent too much time in the sun.

Arnie! Sitting in front of the counter, talking with Amy Thurgood, editor of the *Courier*. A woman in her fifties, she had her glasses perched on top of gray hair.

Dressed in a work shirt and jeans, Arnie turned slowly toward her. His eyes flared momentarily before he could disguise his surprise. "Hey, Ellie." Beside him, Sheila stood and wagged her tail in recognition.

Swallowing hard, Ellie forced herself to regain her composure and walked the rest of the way inside. "Hello, Arnie." Her throat was so tight, her voice rose to a higher pitch than usual.

"What brings you to the hallowed halls of the *Courier*?" he asked.

"I, um, wanted to talk to Amy about the expansion plans for Ability Counts." She placed the file folder of information on the counter.

Lifting her glasses from where they'd been perched on top of her head, Amy flipped open the folder. "I reported the school board turning down the idea of making it a charter school. Vanna's going to expand, anyway?"

"That's the plan. We hope to build some community support before bringing a permit request before the city council."

Adjusting the position of his wheelchair, Arnie tried to read the material in the flyer upside down. "Vanna's one smart lady. I got a pretty lukewarm reception from Ted Rojas when I talked to him last week. A little pressure from the public could nudge him over to our side."

Amy skimmed the statistics about disabled students in the region, then closed the folder.

"So you want me to write an article about how you're moving on without the school board's help?" she asked.

"Plus the importance of the school and how the community can help, if you can work that all in," Ellie said.

Shrugging, Amy glanced at Arnie. "And this guy wants an article about the Paralympics marathon in Bozeman that's a week from Saturday. Looks like I'm going to be spending a lot of time at the computer the next couple of days."

After making her contribution in support of Arnie's race, Ellie had forgotten all about the event. She hadn't even put the date on her calendar.

"We're hoping to get a big turnout of people watching the race," Arnie said. "The wheelchair division starts at eight o'clock. At eight-thirty we've got about a hundred runners signed up to participate—guys and gals with prosthetics, some blind runners with sighted partners. It's going to be quite a scene."

"Is Sheila going to run with you?" Ellie asked.

"No, going that far on mostly asphalt would be too hard on her paws. I'll leave her with Daniel."

Ellie imagined Sheila wouldn't much like that. She was too attached to her master to stay behind when he went riding off on his wheelchair.

"I thought I'd cover the event in person," Amy said. "I'd like to get a few photos of our local athletes. Particularly since I figure Arnie here is a good bet to win his division."

"I'd like to come see the race, too," Ellie said before she stopped to think how Arnie might react.

Arnie's expression clouded and he frowned. "You don't have to do that. You'd be bored standing around for half the morning."

His words grated, and she fought to not lash back at him. "I don't think so."

Despite her vow to keep her distance from Arnie, he wasn't going to stop her from attending the race and cheering for him, win or lose.

With a stifled sigh, she realized down deep that she'd never be able to keep her distance from Arnie.

Chapter Nine

Their business completed at the *Courier,* both Ellie and Arnie decided to leave at the same time.

Arnie tried to do the gentlemanly thing and hold the door open for her. But when he pushed open the door, his chair was in the way and she couldn't get past him.

"Go ahead," she said, holding the door for him. "I've got it."

His awkward exit over the raised threshold made her wince. *The town ought to require businesses to be accessible for handicapped people,* she thought, miffed at the town fathers and the owner of the newspaper.

"Where you off to now?" he asked.

"I have some flyers I want to deliver to local businesses. The school needs their support, too."

"I'm sure Mindy will put up a flyer at Knitting and Notions."

"She's on my list to harass before I pick up Torie from after-school care."

One of his reluctant smiles appeared, the slightest

curve of his lips, which brought a mischievous sparkle to his dark eyes, a look she remembered from their old days together.

His expression grew pensive. "I guess Torie's spent a lot of time with sitters and in day care since she was born."

Ellie tensed. Was he criticizing her and the way she was raising her child? "That's what a working mother has to do. I don't think she's suffered from the experience. In fact, that may be why she's so outgoing."

He held up his hand in defense. "I was just thinking how hard it must be for you, taking care of her on your own. She's a great kid, which means you've done just fine with her."

The unexpected praise caught Ellie off guard. For a moment, tears of gratitude pressed at the back of her eyes. "I do what I have to do. It hasn't always been easy for either of us, but we've made it so far. Now, living with my mother, she can look after Torie if she doesn't want to stay for extended care at school. And, of course, I'm right there at school if Torie needs me during the mornings."

"Sounds like a good arrangement."

"Better than most single mothers have."

"Yeah." He rolled his chair back and forth as though he was indecisive about something.

"Are you headed back to the ranch?" she asked.

His motion halted. "Afraid so. We're culling the herd for winter, and that wallboard isn't smart enough to put itself up. There's always something to do around the ranch."

"Well, then…" She knelt to give Sheila a few scratches behind her ears. "I guess I'll see you around."

When she stood, she was nearly eye to eye with Jeffrey Robbins, who had just come out of the diner next door. Wearing a blue, long-sleeved shirt, matching striped tie and chinos, he looked all business and more than a little slick.

"Well, hello there, Ms. Ellie James," he drawled in a surgary sweet voice. He swept a straying lock of hair off his forehead with his hand. "What a pleasure to see you again."

She greeted him with a simple nod.

"Robbins," Arnie said.

As though the man hadn't noticed Arnie's presence, Robbins shot a surprised look in his direction. "Hey, my man. How's it going?" He extended his hand, and the two men indulged in a silent battle of who had the stronger grip.

"If you two will excuse me," Ellie said. "I've got some things I have to do."

Robbins released his grip. "I hope you've reconsidered my invitation, Ellie. I can promise you a lovely evening."

She gave a quick shake of her head. "Sorry. I'm not interested."

Anger flared in Robbins's eyes.

"The lady said she's not interested, Jeff. So back off and leave her alone."

Sheila, sensing the antagonism between the two men, braced her legs and pulled her lips back into snarl.

Ellie stepped between Arnie and Robbins. In her most stern schoolteacher voice, she said, "That's enough. Both of you are acting like little boys on the playground, fighting over a ball that doesn't belong to either of you. Stop it."

Robbins's head snapped up, and he gaped at Ellie.

Arnie had the good sense to look chagrined.

"I'm sure both of you have business elsewhere." She planted her fists on her hips. "I suggest you leave now."

She stood her ground until Robbins broke eye contact, whirled and marched away. She sighed. *Men!*

"I'm sorry, Ellie." Arnie wheeled closer to her. "I was out of line. I have no right to stick my nose in your business. If you want to date that guy—"

"Arnold O'Brien! Don't you realize you are ten times, a hundred times, more of a man than Jeffrey Robbins is or ever could be? I wouldn't go out with him if he promised to make me the queen of England."

Slack-jawed, Arnie stared at her without uttering a single sound.

Throwing up her arms in frustration, she marched down the sidewalk and into the diner to deliver one of her flyers. What did she have to do to get Arnie to trust her again?

The man was as dense as a fence post and twice as impossible!

She was a fool to even try to get back into his good graces. And an idiot to make the shocking admission, even to herself, that she was falling for him all over again.

Openmouthed, Arnie watched Ellie vanish into the diner. She was the strongest, the toughest woman he'd ever known, and she'd just whupped him and Robbins, but good.

Where had she gained that kind of inner strength? Eight years ago she'd been a beautiful, impulsive bubblehead, or so he'd thought. Boy, had she changed.

Her passionate defense of Ability Counts and her students had made her even more appealing.

He finally snapped his mouth closed.

"Come on, Sheila. Let's go home. We have some serious thinking to do."

Back at the ranch, Arnie joined Daniel, who had already started culling the herd in anticipation of the coming winter, when the grass would be under as much as six feet of snow. Buying expensive winter feed, and getting it to the cattle in a blizzard, wasn't Arnie's idea of a good time. So they kept the herd small during the winter and bought yearlings in the spring to fatten them up.

He rode his ATV, keeping the cattle to be sold off separated from the rest of the herd. Daniel sat astride April, his favorite quarter horse, a sorrel mare with a blond mane. They'd isolated about twenty head, enough for a truckload to be sent to Bozeman.

"Okay," Daniel shouted from the far side of the smaller herd. "Let's move 'em into the pen."

While Daniel kept the herd leader heading in the right direction, Arnie cruised behind the group, the sound of the ATV making the cattle nervous enough that they kept moving. He gestured for Sheila to go after a cow that was trying to wander back to the bigger herd.

Leaping from the ATV, Sheila raced after the recalcitrant animal. She barked and nipped at the cow's hind legs until she reversed course back to where she belonged.

Maybe that was what Ellie was doing to Arnie—dogging his heels until he did exactly what she wanted.

But what did she want?

She'd run out on him eight years ago, abandoning him. Making him feel even more the cripple he'd become. Unworthy of her love.

He frowned. Could he really have told her to go away? Why couldn't he remember? Had he been that much of a fool?

Sheila's assignment accomplished, she jumped back into the ATV and sat up alertly, waiting for her next task.

"Good girl!" Arnie ruffled her fur and patted her rump.

The cattle funneled their way into the pen and milled around while Daniel closed the gate behind them.

He settled on his horse, lightly holding the reins in one hand, and tipped his Stetson to the back of his head. Despite the cool air, his denim jacket hung open. "I'll call the trucking company for a pickup in the morning."

"I hope we get a decent price for them," Arnie said.

"Yeah, me, too. The grass was pretty good this year. They put on some good weight. Luckily, we didn't lose a single head to wolves or mountain lions."

"Which doesn't mean we won't next year."

For a moment, both men admired the cattle they'd raised at the cost of considerable hard work, gallons of sweat and no small amount of the Lord's help.

The blue sky overhead, the sun turning the grass-covered hillsides golden, made for a perfect autumn day to celebrate their accomplishments.

"Tell me something, bro." Thoughtfully, Arnie stroked his dog. "Be straight with me. Do you think a woman would ever want to marry me?"

Hooking his leg over the pommel, Daniel turned in the saddle to look at Arnie. His interested expression lasered in on him, and Arnie hated himself for having brought up the subject.

"Forget about it." Arnie put his hand on the gear to shift the ATV into Reverse, to get out of there. "It was just an idle thought. Didn't mean a thing."

"Now, wait a minute. You can't drop a bomb like that and not tell me what's going on. Give, bro."

"There's no bomb. Nothing's going on. I'm sorry I said anything." He backed in a circle, then headed for home, aiming to get back to work on the wallboard job. Of all the dumb things to say, he'd picked a winner. He should've kept his mouth shut.

Daniel galloped up beside him and shouted over the noise of the ATV. "If you're thinking about Ellie, I'd say marrying her would be the best thing that ever happened to you."

Fear, like a summer twister tearing up the landscape, churned in Arnie's gut. The wind in his face made his eyes water and parched his throat.

He had to wonder, would he be the *worst* thing that ever happened to *her?*

So awful that she would leave him again?

Arnie didn't think he could handle that. It wasn't a risk he wanted to take.

He was better off just as he was. Living on the ranch. Soon in his own house. Alone. With no one around to break his heart again.

Sunday morning, despite her good sense and an hour's worth of lecturing herself about the error of futile thinking, Ellie looked forward to church and to seeing Arnie.

She'd also stopped by to see Pastor Redmond on Saturday to ask him to announce that Ability Counts needed community support for their expansion. She hoped he'd say something from the pulpit. She had flyers with her with information about Vanna's plans.

Choosing to wear a layered look for church, she picked out a lime-green blouse and a knit vest to wear with her smoke-gray skirt. A couple of strokes with her hairbrush, a little lip gloss, and she was ready to go.

After she dropped Torie off in the child-care room, she walked around to the front entrance and found Daniel standing at the door, greeting parishioners as they arrived. Wearing a Western-cut shirt with a bolo tie, he looked very much the gentleman cowboy out on the town. What changes he'd made in his life in the past eight years!

"Hey, Ellie." He handed her a program. "How's it going?"

"Fine. Working hard to stir up community support for expanding Ability Counts."

"Yeah, Mindy said you came by the shop the other day with flyers." He glanced around, and when nobody was close by, he leaned toward Ellie. "Say, are you and Arnie…" His voice dropped below the sound of a breeze slipping through pine trees. "I mean, are you two seeing each other?"

Her cheeks burned with the heat of a thousand-watt lightbulb. She brought the church program to her lips, trying to cover the blazing evidence of her reaction. Evidence that she wished what he had asked was true.

"No!" Her denial was more of a burst of sound than a word. "Not at all. We're both helping Ability Counts, that's all." She shoved one of her flyers toward him.

"Oh." His lips formed a small circle, and his dark brows, so much like his brother's, lowered in what looked like disappointment. "I just wondered…."

She tried to force a smile, but it felt like her cheeks were carved of wood and would crack if she stretched her lips any farther. "See you later."

Her face still radiating heat, she fled into the church. Her mother was there, somewhere, saving her a seat, but Ellie couldn't seem to focus.

What had made Daniel think she was "seeing" Arnie? As in dating? Not a chance.

Scanning the pews, Ellie kept her eye out for her mother. She edged down the aisle and suddenly stumbled into Arnie in his wheelchair, parked at the end of a pew.

"Oh, sorry." Off balance, she grabbed the back of his chair to right herself.

"Easy does it. I'm out of practice having women fall for me." She saw a flash of something in his eyes. Anger that she'd stumbled over him? Or embarrassment that he and his wheelchair were often invisible to others, a frequent problem for those who were wheelchair bound? What a burden that had to be for a man like Arnie.

"Yes, well…" She stepped back. She'd looked forward to seeing Arnie, but not this way. Not by making a fool of herself or a spectacle. Or by hurting him. "Sorry. I wasn't paying attention. I was looking for Mother."

"Three rows down." He lifted his chin in that direction.

"Thanks."

The organist segued from a prelude to the opening hymn. Pastor Redmond walked out onto the stage, and the congregation rose.

Embarrassed by her awkward stumble, Ellie gave Arnie a finger wave and hurried to join her mother, who scooted over to make room for her on the aisle. Barbara held open the hymnal for Ellie to join in singing "Hail, Happy Morning."

The lively song settled Ellie's capricious emotions. By the time the music ended, she felt able to concentrate on the worship service and ignore the niggling awareness of Arnie only three pews behind her.

The pastor stepped up to the pulpit. "Welcome to you all on this happy Sabbath morning. Before I bore you with my sermon…" He got a chuckle from the congregation with that comment. "I have some announcements.

"First, let me remind you about our annual autumn picnic at Riverside Park. The date and time are in your program. Mrs. Green, our lovely women's group president, is organizing a potluck, and the men's group will be arranging games for all ages. We're all hoping for a good turnout and a day of fun and Christian fellowship. We'll caravan from church, so, ladies, don't wear all your finery that morning."

That got another chuckle from the congregation.

Ellie remembered the church's family picnics, staid affairs compared to the afternoons and evenings she'd spent at River Park during her adolescent years. But Torie would enjoy the picnic and the games the children played, and her mother liked visiting with her friends from church.

Next, the pastor told them about Ability Counts and the expansion they were hoping to achieve. His final announcement was about the Paralympics marathon in Bozeman and Arnie's participation.

Under her breath, Barbara said, "I suppose you intend to be there."

Ellie stiffened. "You're welcome to come with me. I thought I'd take Torie, too. She's grown quite fond of Arnie."

Barbara wrinkled her nose.

If only her mother could see Arnie as he truly was, strong and caring, a man who was defined by much more than his paraplegia, perhaps that would change her attitude. But Barbara clung to seeing Arnie as she had seen her late brother, through a distorted lens that showed only the pain and dependency of disability.

With a sad feeling of defeat, Ellie realized there was nothing she could do to change her mother's opinion. It was a wall Barbara had constructed years ago, one that had withstood the test of time and remained impregnable to any argument or logic.

Chapter Ten

"Based on the phone calls I've received this week, I'd say more than a hundred letters supporting our expansion have been sent to the city council." Although Vanna had dark circles of fatigue under her eyes, and there were piles of unfinished paperwork on her desk, she looked more than pleased with their campaign.

"Let's hope the council members listen to their constituents." Ellie had been busy all week and was glad Friday had finally arrived. In addition to her regular teaching assignment and being a parent as well as a daughter, she had attended a meeting of the local women's club to ask for their support. Vanna had been out making contacts, as well.

"Oh, I think we'll do fine," Vanna said.

"We may not get Robbins's vote. I think I really made him angry."

Vanna chuckled. "He'll come around when he sees how the other council members are voting."

From a pewter sky outside Vanna's office, rain dripped from the eaves, making pinging noises when the drops landed on a trash can. Very little light worked its way in through the window. The weather report had called for heavy rain in the nearby mountains, which were tinder-dry after a long summer.

"When will the item be on the agenda?" Ellie asked.

"We'll take another week to build support. I'll ask Mayor Knudsen to put us on the agenda a week from Tuesday." Rubbing her hand along her jaw, she said, "I assume you're going to Bozeman tomorrow to cheer for Arnie."

"Oh, yes. Torie and I will be there." No matter what Arnie said, Ellie had no intention of missing the race, rain or shine. He might become upset seeing her there, but it was one of the few ways she could show how much she cared, how much she'd changed.

"Arnie and the Paralympics have been a great help to us. Once we get the approval to expand, I think they'll play a critical role in developing ongoing funding for us."

That was Ellie's hope, too. But now she had to get to her class. Rain meant no Friday horseback riding for the children, and they'd be restless. She'd have to work at keeping them busy and active. A few rounds of London Bridge and Duck, Duck, Goose would help them use some of their pent-up energy.

By the following morning the storm had passed through the area, leaving only a few trailing clouds and air as crystal clear as a finely cut diamond. Overnight, the temperature had dropped into the low forties.

Both Ellie and Torie were bundled up in warm jackets. Holding her daughter's hand, Ellie worked their way through the milling crowd in the high school stadium to be near the starting line. Excitement and anticipation had Ellie craning her neck to get a glimpse of Arnie. She so wanted him to do well in the race.

"Can you see Arnie?" Torie kept bouncing up on her tiptoes to get a better view.

"Not yet." There were dozens of men and a few women in sleek racing wheelchairs jockeying for position on the tartan running track, each of them with a number bib pinned to their back. "I wish I knew what number he was wearing."

"There's Sheila!" Torie pointed to the far side of the track, where Daniel had the golden retriever mix on a leash. That had to mean Arnie was nearby.

Ellie scanned the racers close to Daniel.

"There he is." Her excitement rising, she squatted down next to Torie and pointed. "He's right up front, wearing a bright red track shirt and blue shorts. His cap is red, too. Do you see him?"

It took Torie just a moment to spot him. "Arnie! Arnie!" She waved her arm and jumped up and down. "We came to see you race."

He turned his head slowly. When he pinpointed Torie, a smile of recognition softened his angular features, and he waved.

"He sees me, Mommy. He sees me. Can I go talk to him?"

"No, honey. We don't want to distract him. He needs to concentrate on the race." What Ellie really wanted to do was race across the track to give Arnie a good-luck kiss. The thought of getting a negative reception, should she actually do that, kept the impulse in check.

Torie's slender shoulders sagged. "I could help him concentrate."

Ellie hooked her arm around her daughter's shoulders. "Not this time. After the race is over, you'll have a chance to talk to him."

"Is he going to win?"

Arnie turned to say something to Daniel. Ellie noted his racer's number was 314.

"I don't know," she said to Torie. "He's going to do his best, though. You can be sure of that." Although not as reckless as his brother, Arnie had always had fire in his belly when it came to competition. He'd been a star high school football player and had set some Potter Creek track records. Long before Ellie knew him. Before his accident.

The accident that had demolished much of what Arnie's self-image had been. Yet he was still a competitor. Even from a distance, she saw his grim determination. His intense concentration. His will to win.

He'd put that same resolve into restoring the ranch to a productive enterprise. Being in a wheelchair hadn't deterred him. So why couldn't she convince him being wheelchair bound didn't make her think less of him?

A race official raised his starting pistol. "Ready, set—"

Ellie jumped at the sound of the gun. Her heart slammed against her rib cage, and she drew a quick breath.

The racers sped forward at an amazing pace, maneuvering for position, their arms pumping hard. The onlookers cheered.

"I can't see, Mommy. I can't see."

Ellie hefted her daughter in her arms. She focused on Arnie's red cap and shirt as he kept his position at the front of the pack. Two other racers were neck and neck with him going down the track to the first turn, Arnie on the outside, trying to pass them.

That was a mistake, she thought. He should be on the inside of the turn, with the shorter distance to travel.

Unlike a speed ice-skating track or one used for race cars, a running track wasn't banked. The inside racer reached the turn going too fast. His chair tipped precariously. He was forced to slow.

On the outside, Arnie zipped by his two rivals and sped on alone.

"Go, Arnie! Go!" Ellie screamed.

Torie covered her ears. "That's too loud, Mommy."

Laughing, Ellie lowered her daughter to the ground as the racers peeled away from the track, out an open gate and onto the street to follow the twenty-six-mile course.

"When will Arnie come back, Mommy?"

She glanced toward Daniel across the way. "I don't

really know. It's a long race. Probably more than an hour."

Many of the racers were young, in their early twenties. Most of them were probably accident victims or soldiers injured in the line of duty. All of them had had to rebuild their lives under the most difficult of circumstances.

I should have been there for Arnie, she thought. Dealing with such a devastating change in his life must have been terrible for him. If only he'd asked her to stay…

Ellie and Torie moved with the crowd to watch the racers pass on the nearby street. They found a spot to stand on the sidewalk among the fans, mostly friends and family members of the racers.

The ripple of applause and cheers started somewhere to Ellie's right. Like a fast-approaching train, the noise grew closer until she could see those in the lead.

Arnie wasn't among them.

She craned her neck until she spotted him in fifth place and still in contact with the leaders, who were traveling a good thirty miles per hour.

"Come on, Arnie! You can do it." She pointed for Torie. "There he is."

"He's not winning," Torie complained.

"Don't you worry, young lady," a woman next to them said. "He's saving his strength by drafting behind the racer in front of him. He'll catch up at the end. That's my boy right behind him."

Although Ellie didn't think winning was the most

important thing about any race, she couldn't help hoping Arnie would come in first at the finish line.

The wheelchair racers had barely passed when the crowd surged back into the stadium to watch the runners make their start. Ellie looked on in amazement as men and women with prosthetic legs, some even using crutches, accepted the challenge of running 26.2 miles.

She doubted she could finish a 10K race with two good legs, much less a marathon.

After the runners left the stadium, the time seemed to drag. Ellie checked her watch. The crowd collected on the infield grass near the finish line the racers would cross after returning to the stadium and circling the quarter-mile track.

She pictured Arnie. The muscles in his arms flexing with each pull of the wheels, his shoulders as broad and strong as those of a wrestler. His expression intent as he focused every ounce of his energy on the race.

Finally, a collective gasp rose from the onlookers as the first two racers rolled onto the track, followed closely by a third.

Her heart slammed to a stop when she recognized Arnie's red cap in third place.

Without giving it any thought, Ellie raced across the grass, angling toward Arnie and the lead racers. Right behind her, Torie yelled, "Wait, Mommy!"

Ellie grabbed her child's hand and kept on running.

"Come on, Arnie! You can do it! It's not far now. Keep going. Faster, Arnie!" Ellie's screams, rasping up her throat, strained her vocal cords, but she didn't stop.

Arnie closed the distance on the other two racers. Sweat ran down his face and soaked the back of his red shirt. With every turn of the wheels, he seemed to find a little more strength, apply a bit more power.

Torie added her shouts of encouragement as Arnie pulled to the outside lane to pass the competition.

The racer on the inside was having trouble holding his lane again. A rear wheel wobbled off the tartan track, banged against the low curb, costing him precious time.

Arnie took advantage of the error. He pressed into second place. Determination was written in the grimace of his mouth, the corded muscles of his neck and the way he leaned forward to get as much leverage as possible.

When they reached the straightaway, Arnie was only inches behind the leader. The crowd began to roar.

Touching the cross around her neck, Ellie closed her eyes only long enough to send up a quick prayer. When she opened them again, the two men were dead even and about to cross the finish line. Both men were working so hard, it was impossible to imagine them having an extra ounce of strength left.

A huge cheer went up from the onlookers.

"Who won, Mommy?"

"I don't know, honey. I can't see." Wheelchair racers continued to whiz by. The first woman finished in the middle of a pack of male racers, receiving another loud cheer.

Picking Torie up, Ellie forced her way through the crowd, past the finish line, to the spot where the racers were recovering their breath. She had to find out who had won.

When she reached the recovery area, she saw Arnie. He was congratulating a muscular young man who was waving an American flag high in the air, a big grin on his face.

The air escaped Ellie's lungs in a sigh. Arnie had placed second. An incredibly good showing against a strong field of racers.

With dozens of people greeting the racers they had cheered for, Ellie walked across the track. She lowered Torie to the ground.

"You were wonderful." Her voice sounded like she had a frog in her throat.

His hair damp with perspiration, his smile a little crooked, he beckoned her closer. He took Ellie's hand, tugging her onto his lap. His big, work-roughened hands framed her face.

She gasped with surprise and pleasure, his thighs firmly beneath her.

"I tried to win for you. I heard you yelling. I didn't want to let you down. Disappoint you. I'm sorry."

"Nothing you ever did would disappoint me, Arnie."

Slowly, not sure what his reaction would be, she brought her lips to his. Warm and familiar, she remembered his kisses. Longed for them. For a moment, he didn't respond, and then he relaxed. He kissed her back. She wanted to weep with the simple pleasure of being in his arms again.

"Mommy, can I sit in Arnie's lap, too?"

Reluctantly, Ellie broke away from the kiss. His dark eyes were as heated as his kiss had been. As needy as her own desire.

An unspoken message passed between them, bringing the past and the present together. A clash of lost love and broken trust.

This had been their first kiss in eight years, but would it be their last?

"Mom-my! It's my turn."

With a troubled smile, Ellie eased off of his lap.

Arnie shifted his attention to Torie. "Come on, squirt. Come up here and give me a high five."

"I cheered for you, Arnie."

"I know you did, squirt. Sorry I didn't win for you."

"But you did win. Mommy says when you try your best, you'll always be a winner."

He shrugged and gave her a high five. "If you say so, kiddo."

Others began to gather around Arnie. People from Potter Creek—Vanna and Ivy from the diner, Daniel returning Sheila to his side and draping a jacket around Arnie's shoulders so he wouldn't cool off too fast. Pastor Redmond congratulated him on his second-place finish, as did several members of his congregation. Others gathered around him were his friends from

Paralympics and who knew where else. He was a popular guy.

He greeted everyone with a handshake or a hug, and regret that he hadn't won first place.

But the kiss had been Ellie's alone.

Suddenly, heat warmed her cheeks. All these people, Arnie's friends, must have seen her kissing him. But no one commented, for which Ellie was ever so grateful. She should have restrained herself in such a public setting but was so glad she hadn't.

After the runners had finished their race, officials of the Bozeman Paralympics made the presentation of awards. Arnie received a large gold trophy, and the young man who had beaten him accepted a trophy that was at least two feet tall.

"Ladies and gentlemen," the official announced over the loudspeaker. "Even more important than this race is the fact that more than $20,000 has been pledged for the support of our organization. I'd like to recognize our top fundraiser, who, all by himself, collected pledges of $3,253.10." The audience chuckled at the ten cents. "Let's give him a big hand, folks. Arnie O'Brien, our second-place finisher."

Pride filled Ellie's chest as the official draped a gold medal around Arnie's neck. Life was about a lot more than simply winning a race.

It was about caring and giving back. How could she not love a man like Arnie?

Chapter Eleven

The row of spruce trees bordering the highway back to the ranch leaned to the west, victims of the frequent winds that blew through the area, stunting their growth, twisting their limbs. Making them less than perfect.

It was just as well Daniel had decided to drive the van back to the ranch after the race. Arnie figured even with power steering, he wouldn't have been able to get out of the parking lot.

He could barely hold on to the trophy he'd won for second place, the figure of a wheelchair racer on the top.

His arms had as much strength left in them as a gym towel that had been dropped in the deep end of the pool. Exertion had drained his energy. He'd downed three bottles of water to rehydrate. During the race, he had expended every ounce of strength he had, yet he was still on an adrenaline high.

From Ellie's kiss.

"You ran quite a race, bro," Daniel said.

"I had a good coach. I should've done better." During the final quarter mile he'd heard Ellie's voice above all the other screaming fans. He'd wanted to slow down. His energy depleted, he hadn't wanted to push any harder. Finishing in third place wouldn't be so bad, he had told his weary body.

But he couldn't do that. Not with Ellie's voice in his head, urging him to go faster, push harder. Win. Because of Ellie, he had come so close.

How had she known he had more left in him when he hadn't known it himself? When he'd been ready to quit trying.

An errant thought popped into his head. Had he given up on Ellie too soon? When he'd gotten out of rehab, why hadn't he gone after her?

The answer came to him like a sucker punch to his chin. *Because you were too afraid she'd say no.* Better to blame her than discover what he feared the most, that she couldn't love a cripple.

"That was quite a congratulatory kiss you got from Ellie," Daniel said. "Looked like you were both into it."

"Yeah. Felt like it, too," he admitted. He'd been hungry for that kiss since she'd come back to town. Yearning to feel the old fire ignite between them.

Yet it had been more than before. Better than before. How could he not want to kiss her again?

He didn't dare. The kiss had changed nothing.

He was still too afraid to find out the truth. To test the limits of how she felt about him.

* * *

Unsettled by Arnie's kiss, Ellie drove home from Bozeman, barely hearing Torie chattering away in the backseat of her compact.

She parked by the back door of her mother's house. As usual, Torie blasted out of the car as though she was rocket-propelled.

Sitting for a moment behind the steering wheel, Ellie touched her fingertips to her lips. The feel of him, the press of his lips, still lingered there.

Dazed, she walked up the steps into the kitchen, where Torie was regaling her grandmother with the details of the race.

"…was losing. But Mommy kept yelling at him to go faster, and so did I. We ran and ran to keep up with him. Then he started rolling faster and faster, and he just about caught up with the other man!"

"Just about, huh? Goodness, that sounds like an exciting race," Grandma BarBar said.

"He got a great big, gigantic trophy that was bigger than me." Torie held her hand high above her head.

Chuckling, Ellie slipped off her jacket. "Maybe not quite that big."

"But it was really, really big," Torie insisted.

"Oh, yes. They don't come much bigger." Ellie helped her daughter take off her jacket.

"After Arnie finished the race, Mommy sat in his lap and kissed him for a long time."

Ellie winced. There were no secrets as far as a talkative four-year-old was concerned.

Her mother shot her a stinging look.

"Then she had to give me a turn," Torie continued, "so I sat in his lap and gave him a high five."

Her jaw muscles taut, Barbara said, "I see."

Immediately jumping to defend Arnie, Ellie said, "You really should have seen him, Mother. Arnie is so incredibly strong and vigorous. Well, all the racers were, of course. But he was flying."

With a dismissive wave of her hand, Barbara stood. "I'll fix us some nice hot soup and tuna sandwiches for lunch."

Torie wrinkled her nose. "I don't like tuna. Can I have peanut butter?"

"Remember, honey, at Grandma's house we eat what we're served. And after you eat your lunch, you and I are going to plan who to invite to your birthday party."

Her complaint deflected, Torie clapped her hands. "I'm going to be five years old."

"You certainly are." Barbara popped open a can of chicken noodle soup and poured it into a pan. "How did you get to be such a grown-up little girl?"

"'Cuz my mommy borned me."

And what a long way they'd come since then, Ellie thought. Her mother had come to Spokane to be with her when she gave birth. Barbara hadn't been happy about Ellie being an unwed mother, but she'd been as supportive as she knew how. She'd stayed a week to help Ellie recover; then she'd returned to the farm, leaving Ellie on her own. Trying to keep up with her classes that semester and care for a new baby hadn't been easy.

Overall, it had been worth every sleepless night and blurry-eyed morning.

Returning to her job as a waitress after six weeks had compounded her lack of sleep. Even so, she'd survived and baby Victoria Barbara James had thrived. At first a kind neighbor lady had taken care of Torie when Ellie was at work or school. Later, Ellie was able to use the child-care program available to faculty and students, sponsored by the university.

Barbara continued to be supportive and was more than loving with Torie when Ellie came home for brief visits.

But she had a blind spot when it came to Arnie.

A blind spot that hurt Ellie in a deeply visceral way.

After lunch, Ellie cleared the dishes and put them in the dishwasher, while her mother went off to take a nap.

Finding some notebook paper, Ellie sat down at the table again. "All right, Miss Birthday Girl. Who should we invite to your party?"

After some discussion, Torie agreed she should invite all the children in her class.

"And I want to invite Arnie, too," she announced.

Ellie's pencil froze above the lined paper. "Honey, he's a grown-up. I'm not sure he'd want to come to a party with so many kids."

"But he's my very, very best grown-up friend."

"Well, yes…" She mentally scrambled to come up with a reason not to invite Arnie, when in her heart she would love to have him here. Torie needed a man in her life as a role model. But would Arnie feel she was taking advantage of him, pressuring him to deepen their relationship? Assuming one kiss made theirs a relationship.

"You could ask him, Mommy." Her green eyes were round and big and pleading.

Rubbing her forehead, Ellie considered her options. "Tell you what, why don't we invite Arnie, Daniel and Mindy to the party? They've all been very nice to us, and that way there would be other grown-ups to talk to."

"Okay," she agreed brightly.

Together they planned a cowboy theme and the games the children would play. Grandma BarBar would be asked to make a chocolate cake and serve ice cream.

Hugging her daughter, Ellie thought of all the preparations she needed to make before next Saturday, and her stomach sank. She should have started planning a month ago.

With her computer-generated party invitations in hand, Ellie made sure to get to church early the next morning and drop off Torie in her Sunday school room. She'd either catch the O'Briens before church started or track them down after the service.

For once, her timing was perfect. Arnie's van was just pulling into the parking lot as she reached the front of the church. She waited for him on the sidewalk and watched as Mindy and Daniel exited the van, as well.

Asking all three of them to the party made the invitation seem less pushy. Less personal.

And much easier for Arnie to decline.

"Hey, we've got our own personal greeter this morning." Tipping his hat back, Daniel strolled toward Ellie, and she remembered how she and Mindy used to call him Swagger.

"I'm here at Torie's behest to deliver some special invitations to all the O'Briens."

"Oh, oh." Arnie rolled up to her. "That sounds like trouble to me."

"Oh, hush, Arnie." Mindy whopped him lightly on the shoulder. "Torie's a sweet girl and you know it."

Ellie's gaze locked on Arnie's, his pupils as dark as charcoal. Her mouth dry, she couldn't look away. He was remembering their kiss, just as she was. Her stomach did a flip-flop, and her chest tightened.

"So what are we invited to?" Daniel asked.

The question snapped Ellie out of her reverie. "Torie's birthday party is next Saturday. She wanted you all to come, if you can." She handed them their invitations.

"Oh, how sweet." Mindy opened hers. "A cowboy theme. I remember my son's second birthday. I had broomstick horses for all the children. They galloped all over the house."

Ellie's heart squeezed tight in sympathy. She couldn't imagine the pain her friend must have suffered when she lost her son.

Daniel put a protective arm around his wife's shoulders. "Losing Jason is the reason we wanted to get started on our family as soon as possible."

"You'll notice my brother was glad to oblige," Arnie teased.

Daniel ignored him.

"I'd love to help you with the party," Mindy said, obviously not wanting to dwell on the loss of her child. "I could find some cute fabric and stitch up some bandannas for the children to wear around their necks."

"That would be perfect," Ellie said.

The sound of the organ prelude wafted out from the church.

"I'll give you a call," Mindy said. "We'll talk about how else I can help. And I'll ask Aunt Martha to watch the shop that afternoon."

"Thank you so much."

Taking Mindy's arm, Daniel headed toward the church entrance. Arnie started to follow them, but Ellie stopped him.

"Please don't feel you have to come to the party," she said. "It was Torie's idea to invite you. She says, and I quote, 'Arnie is my very, very best grown-up friend.'"

Cocking his head, he looked up at her. "You don't want me there?"

She flushed. "Of course I do. I can't think of anyone else I'd rather have come to the party. It's just that..." Her tongue suddenly as thick as a tree stump, she stumbled over her words. "After yesterday, I don't want you to feel you have any obligation to me. Or to Torie."

Slowly, his lips curved into a reluctant smile and

crinkles appeared at the corners of his eyes. "No obligation. I get that."

The deep timbre of his voice vibrated in the air between them and resonated in her chest. More than anything, she wanted to kiss him again. Right there. In front of the church. She didn't care who saw them. But his tone didn't invite a repeat of yesterday's kiss.

"Tell Torie I'm happy to accept her invitation."

As he wheeled into church, Ellie wondered if Arnie had had birthday parties as a child. His mother had died when he and Daniel were quite young. His father had had a reputation as a drunk who got into fights, and had allowed the ranch to run down. If there had been parties for the boys, there hadn't been many.

Her heart ached for what Arnie must have missed as a child and what he had accomplished despite a father who likely neglected him or worse.

She wondered if he was aware of what he'd overcome. Or did he simply take life one day at a time?

Chapter Twelve

"Mommy, is it time to get up yet?"

Ellie peeked open one eye. Torie stood next to her bed in her princess pajamas. Outside it was still dark. The clock on her bed table read 5:32 a.m.

Groaning, Ellie pulled back the covers and patted the space beside her. "Not yet, honey. Climb in. Maybe we can get some more sleep."

"But I don't want to miss my birthday."

"You won't, I promise."

Torie got into bed, snuggling her warm little body next to Ellie. She pulled the blanket up over them, catching the fresh scent of baby shampoo on Torie's hair. She wondered how many years it would be before Torie no longer would want to climb into bed with her. She'd be too grown-up.

By six o'clock, Torie was squirming so much it seemed pointless to remain in bed, despite the fact that the party didn't start until one. The weatherman had predicted rain, late afternoon or evening. Ellie hoped it would hold off until after the party.

They both dressed in jeans and flannel shirts. Ellie wore her old scuffed and worn cowboy boots; Torie a red cowboy hat Grandma BarBar had purchased at the party store.

Ellie had the tables covered and bales of hay arranged in the barn when Mindy arrived early to help with the setup. She had her blond hair pulled back into a ponytail. That would have made her look years younger except for her maternity top with a circular target on it, an arrow pointing directly at the bull's-eye, and the word *baby* written under it.

Torie came running out of the house to see what Mindy had brought.

"I found some cute fabric for the bandannas," Mindy announced, placing a cardboard box filled with red-checkered material with tiny horseshoes on the table.

Climbing up on the bench, Torie snatched a bandanna from the box. "Can I wear one now?"

With a silent eye roll, Ellie tied the bandanna in place.

Together, Ellie and Mindy strung crepe paper streamers around the unused horse stalls and set out paper plates and cups. They were contemplating how to tie a rope over a beam to raise and lower the piñata when Daniel and Arnie arrived. Both were dressed in new blue jeans and wearing their Stetsons.

"Ah, the cavalry has arrived," Mindy said with a smile.

When Daniel brushed a kiss to Mindy's cheek, Ellie felt a prick of envy. How lucky her friend was to have rediscovered love.

Arnie rolled into the barn right behind Daniel. "Sounds like we've got a couple of damsels in distress who need rescuing."

"My favorite thing to do." Daniel winked at his wife. "Assuming it's the right woman."

"It better not be any other woman," Mindy warned in a stern voice that contrasted to the hint of laughter in her blue eyes.

Torie came running out of the house, her red hat bouncing on her back from the cord around her neck. "You came to my birthday party!" She flew into Arnie's lap and kissed him on the cheek.

"Hey, squirt. That's some welcome you're giving this ol' cowboy. Happy birthday."

"You're not old, Arnie. You're just right."

Pressing her lips together, Ellie was tempted to agree with her daughter but thought Arnie might not appreciate her opinion in the matter.

"So what do you need?" Arnie asked Ellie, Torie now seated comfortably on his knee, as though she had always belonged there.

Ellie had been hugging the papier-mâché piñata, which was shaped like a horse. "We need a rope strung over a beam so we can hang this."

"No problem." He eyed the beam, which had to be ten feet high. "I'll hold the piñata. My little brother will climb up and risk his neck for the good of the cause."

With a start, Ellie wondered if she'd hurt Arnie, forcing him to silently acknowledge he wasn't able to climb at all. Did he focus on his disabilities, and not all the abilities he still could claim? She pulled her lip between her teeth and prayed that wasn't the case.

"I can climb up there, Mommy."

"Oh, no," Daniel said. He swept off his Stetson and bowed to Torie. "It is my duty as a cowboy to protect all females from possible harm."

The child folded her arms across her chest. "I'm not a female! I'm a little girl!"

Laughter broke the undertone of tension that was always present between Ellie and Arnie. When he gave Torie another affectionate hug, his eyes were on Ellie and his smile warmed her deep in her heart.

Everything was in order when the first children began arriving. Ellie greeted the children and their parents, meeting a few of their chauffeur fathers for the first time.

With a bit too much eagerness and not enough gratitude, Torie took the presents they brought and piled them on top of the table. Typical behavior for a five-year-old, Ellie assumed.

Her mother came out to the barn and organized Pin the Tail on the Donkey, while Mindy tied bandannas around the necks of arriving youngsters and supervised the children who wanted to decorate their pretend vests made out of brown paper sacks.

A scream raised the hair on Ellie's neck. She whirled, expecting to see an injured child.

Instead she saw Arnie and Carson racing their wheelchairs through the barn and out onto the asphalt driveway. The childish scream had been one of laughter as Arnie kept threatening to beat young Carson.

"I'm gonna get you, kid. Look out!"

"I'm faster than you."

"No, you're not." Intentionally staying behind the boy, Arnie gave Carson's chair an extra push. "Hey, no fair. Come back here."

Carson squealed, zipping farther into the lead.

Pulling to a stop, Arnie turned around, a big grin on his face. He rolled back toward the barn, the picture of a mischievous, overgrown boy having fun at a party.

Laughing, Ellie thought that even if Arnie hadn't been given many birthday parties of his own, he certainly knew how to create fun for the children now. Eight years ago, she hadn't known or wondered how good he would be with kids. *Pretty spectacular,* she thought now. He would make a wonderful father—if he ever gave himself a chance.

"Arnie! Arnie!" Torie went running out to him. "Give me a ride, Arnie."

Seeking approval, he glanced toward Ellie, who shrugged. "Up to you."

"Okay, Miss Birthday Girl. I'll give everybody a ride. You first." He hefted Torie up into his lap and wheeled around. "Let's go get Carson."

Soon the children were lined up to take a turn in Arnie's wheelchair and he'd broken into a sweat from exertion. The kids were having so much fun, Ellie hated to stop them.

"They're loving it, aren't they?" Barbara commented, her tone mildly surprised.

"At the moment it's better than riding a horse, which the children adore."

Ellie waited until all the children had had a turn, then gathered them around while Torie opened her presents. Dutifully, Torie thanked whoever had given her a present but didn't linger long over any one gift. She was too anxious to open the next package.

Watching from a few feet away, Arnie downed a large glass of punch.

"I didn't mean for you to be the day's entertainment, but thank you. You were a real hit with the children," Ellie told him.

He pulled a handkerchief from his pocket to wipe the sweat from his brow. His crooked smile made him look bemused. "If I'd trained with one of those kids in my lap, I might've won the marathon."

"There's always next year."

He groaned in mock agony. "Those kids will weigh ten pounds more by next year."

Laughter bubbled out of Ellie like fizzy water. Over the years, she'd forgotten what an understated sense of humor he had, often making her giggle like the teenager she'd been.

She wanted to go back to that time when they laughed together. When they'd been eager to spend time together simply because they liked each other. A lot, from Ellie's perspective.

But going back wasn't an option. Things had changed. So had their relationship. Could they possibly rebuild what they'd once had after so much time had passed? So many hurts had been inflicted.

After the presents were done, Barbara brought out the cake. Ellie snapped a picture when Torie, with a little help from her friends, blew out the five candles.

Thank you, Lord, for my beautiful daughter and the memories she will have of this day.

Barbara helped serve the cake and ice cream. Ellie poured the punch. Too excited to eat, most of the children didn't finish their cake.

After more games and the grand finale of breaking open the piñata, the children finally left.

Ellie sat down heavily on the picnic table bench. Her mother had taken the remnants of the cake inside, and only the O'Briens remained in the barn.

"I can't tell you how grateful I am for all of your help," she said. "I could not have done this without you. I owe you big-time."

"I expect to see you at my little one's first birthday." Mindy patted the bull's-eye on her stomach.

"I'll be there, I promise."

Arnie spun his chair around. "I haven't had such a great workout since the marathon. Can we do this again next week?"

"No!" they all chorused, which was followed by laughter, hugs of gratitude and goodbyes.

* * *

After dinner and getting Torie to bed, Ellie sat in the living room with her mother. She picked up the sweater she was knitting for Torie. If she didn't get busy soon, the sweater wouldn't be finished before next summer.

The rain had held off until evening. Now there was a steady drumming on the roof. Windows rattled when the wind gusted, and a cold draft crept across the floor.

Ellie folded her legs under her.

When the program her mother had been watching on TV ended, Barbara muted the sound.

"I have to say, Arnie was very good with the children today." Her pensive tone caught Ellie's attention.

She looked up from her knitting. "He seemed to be having a good time."

"You know, I always did like him when you were dating him before you moved to Spokane. He was such a responsible young man."

"He still is."

"It's just that—"

"I know, Mother. I remember how painful it was for you to watch Uncle Bob being teased by other children and bullied. But that doesn't happen to Arnie. Everyone in town respects him. Even admires him." Tired of fighting her mother about Arnie, she drew in a shaky breath. "The children think he's wonderful." So did Ellie.

Despite the rain, after dinner Arnie put on a jacket and went out to his house to check what progress his friends had made while he was at Torie's birthday party.

He switched on the floodlight in the living room. Sheila gave herself a shake from nose to tail, spraying water on the unfinished subflooring. The rain beat against the plastic covering on the windows in a futile effort to slip inside the house.

Little Torie had done a great job of slipping under Arnie's skin. Her smile, her laugh, her quick intelligence had opened him up as nothing else had ever done.

Except her mother.

Ellie was doing a number on him, too. He'd thought he could keep being angry at her for walking out on him when he needed her. But every time he saw her, she managed to whittle another small piece of his fury away. The shield he'd hidden behind had become thinner and less substantial by the day.

What would happen if he lowered his defenses? Would everyone see how weak he was? Would Ellie realize what he'd been telling himself all these years was true—that he was only half a man?

He rolled down the hallway to the master bedroom. A room big enough for two. In his imagination he heard Ellie's laughter, caught the scent of her citrus shampoo. Saw her smiling at him.

He scrubbed his hand over his face. It did nothing to erase the image he'd vividly conjured in his head.

"Come on, Sheila. Let's get back to the main house. Mooning over a woman and what could've been isn't going to get me anywhere."

Chapter Thirteen

Soon after Ellie had dismissed her preschool class to go home at noon on Monday, Jeffrey Robbins strolled into her classroom. Wearing an expensive leather jacket and slacks, he looked as out of place in a preschool classroom as a shady bill collector in church.

"So how were all your runny-nosed kids today?" He picked up a painting that had been left on the table to dry, the colors swirled together like a bright rainbow. "Not exactly a Rembrandt, is it?"

Instinctively, Ellie wanted to lash out in defense of her student. Instead she folded her arms across her chest and muted her response.

"I'm sorry," she said, lacing the words with false sympathy. "You must have said something that cruel because your mother burned all of your early paintings."

A quick frown lowered his brows as he struggled to find a suitable comeback. "Fortunately, I have other talents."

"I'm sure." She took the painting from him, returning it to the table where he'd found it. Robbins obviously had a far different attitude toward children than Arnie. He would never have insulted a child's painting or expressed anything except praise. "Is there something you wanted other than a course in art appreciation?"

"Oh, yes, I definitely have something else in mind." He strolled around the room, touching books and toys, examining oversize construction blocks, sliding chairs under tables, marking the space as his own, giving Ellie a creepy feeling in the process.

Tapping her foot, Ellie waited. Although she wanted in the worst way to throw him out, Robbins was a member of the city council. No need to antagonize him more than she already had.

He stopped in the center of the reading circle. "I noticed Ability Counts's request for a building permit is on the city council agenda for tomorrow evening. I thought I'd give you one more chance to discuss the merits of the proposal over dinner this evening."

The man was more determined than she'd imagined. "I have other plans."

"With O'Brien?"

"That's no concern of yours. Now, if you'll excuse me." She looked pointedly toward the door.

Sliding his hands in his pockets, he rocked back on his heels. "Ms. James, I'm in a position to help you."

Said the spider to the fly.

"I appreciate your invitation, Mr. Robbins. While I

must decline, I will look forward to seeing you at the council meeting."

His back straightened, and he removed his hands from his pockets, no longer making an effort to appear relaxed. "You're making a big mistake."

He marched past her and out the door.

The fine hairs on Ellie's nape quivered, as though she were in an electric storm. Goose bumps sped down her spine.

What could he do? Vanna was sure she had enough council votes to have the permit approved. Robbins's negative vote wouldn't matter.

Unless he could convince three other council members to vote no.

Late Tuesday afternoon, while out checking the herd, Arnie got a call from his business associate on the Potter Creek City Council, Ted Rojas.

Slowing his ATV to a stop, Arnie flipped open his cell phone.

"Are you planning to come to the council meeting tonight?" Rojas asked.

"Yeah. Ability Counts's permit is on the agenda tonight, right?"

"Yes, which is why I thought you'd want to know about the email that's been circulating around town. Everybody in city hall and most of the town residents have gotten it."

A sense of alarm caused Arnie to straighten in his seat. "What email?"

"The one that suggests one or more teachers at Ability Counts do not have sufficiently high morals to work with young children and that Vanna should strictly enforce the morals clause in the teachers' contracts before she is allowed to expand the school."

Arnie's hand tightened around the phone. "Who sent it?"

"Councilman Robbins. The memo is long on innuendo and short on facts, but I've already gotten a couple of calls from concerned citizens."

"Send it to me, will you, Ted?" Since the ranch wasn't within the town boundaries, Arnie wasn't a registered voter for city issues and didn't get automatic notification of council agenda items.

"I'll forward it now. If you get a clue about what's going on, let me know."

"You got it." Having a pretty good idea why Robbins sent out the email, Arnie snapped the phone shut. A muscle pulsed in his jaw. He hit the accelerator so hard, he almost dumped Sheila off the back of the ATV.

"Hang on, Sheila. We've got a political mud-throwing contest on our hands." If he had his way, the only guy who would get dirty was Jeffrey Robbins.

Back at the house, Arnie headed directly for his computer. He booted it up and clicked on the email Ted had sent him.

It has been brought to our attention that one or more current teachers at Ability Counts Preschool may have violated the morals clause in the contract they are required to sign at the time they accept employment with the nonprofit organization.

While expansion of the school may or may not be approved, based on the city's land-use plan, we believe it is imperative that Ms. Vanna Coulter, president and CEO of the organization, strictly enforce the morals clause prior to any city council consideration of the request for expansion.

The letterhead on the email indicated it was from the office of Councilman Jeffrey Robbins.

Nearly snarling with fury, Arnie called Vanna and found that she'd already gotten some irate phone calls herself.

"Ellie told me about his implied threat," Vanna said. "Even I didn't think he'd stoop this low."

"He's a snake and always has been. I can't figure out why the voters don't know that." Which didn't mean Ellie should have to sit through a council meeting and be dragged through the mud with him. "Maybe Ellie should skip the council meeting and let us handle it."

"I've already suggested that to her, but she'll have none of it. In fact, since Robbins didn't name names, all of my teachers are upset and in a fighting mood. They plan to stick together and face down Robbins."

Arnie wished them luck. But a guy like Robbins didn't give in easily, not with his ego. He'd have plenty of mud to sling at Ellie, and some of it was bound to stick, at least with some members of the community.

Her reputation would be ruined. She might have to move away from Potter Creek, find a job somewhere else.

Please, God, don't let that happen.

Past Sins Revealed.

Her stomach churning with dread and her fingers trembling, Ellie pictured tomorrow's headline in the *Potter Creek Courier.*

She dressed in her most conservative navy-blue suit. She'd face her accusers. The whole town, if need be. But she wouldn't back down from Jeffrey Robbins.

And her actions could destroy any chance that Ability Counts could expand its program.

Torie hopped up to sit on Ellie's bed. She swung her legs back and forth, bumping against the mattress and springs. "Can I go to the city council with you?"

"No, honey. It's just a boring old meeting." Less boring than usual, from Ellie's perspective. "You wouldn't have any fun."

"Will Arnie be there?"

Standing in front of the full-length mirror in her bedroom, Ellie froze in place. The thought of Arnie hearing a recitation of the sins of her past propelled bile to her throat. She swallowed hard. How could Robbins have discovered details of her years in Spokane?

But Arnie already knew she'd had a child out of wedlock. What more could Robbins dig up—or make up—about her time in Spokane? Would Arnie believe lies about her?

"I don't know if Arnie will be there." She picked up her purse. "Tomorrow's a school day, sweetie. You be sure to be good for Grandma BarBar and go to bed when she tells you to."

When Ellie arrived at city hall, the parking lot was nearly full. She wondered if the crowd was there to support Ability Counts. Or drive an immoral woman from their midst?

Maybe some clever entrepreneur had developed a thriving business selling scarlet letters.

Once inside, Ellie saw the number of parents there to support Ability Counts, and the presence of her fellow teachers bolstered her spirits.

The knowing, sideways glances from others in the audience shook her resolve.

The seven members of the city council took their seats just as Arnie rolled down the aisle and parked his wheelchair next to Ellie.

He gave her hand a squeeze. "Don't worry. Jeff's a master at bluffing. He won't sway anyone."

Arnie's words and the warmth of his hand holding hers restored Ellie's optimism but did nothing to soothe the anxiety ripping holes in her stomach.

Mayor Knudsen, a brawny man who owned the lumberyard in town, called the meeting to order and made quick work of the routine matters on the agenda. Then he called for discussion about Ability Counts's request.

Robbins switched his microphone on and addressed the audience. "I'm sure we all support Miss Vanna's school and the services it provides, particularly for disabled children in the area. However, it is with regret that I feel it necessary to inform you that some questions about the moral character of her staff have been raised. I feel those concerns should be addressed before approving their expansion request."

The mayor interrupted. "Mr. Robbins, you'll need to be more specific. We can't act on vague accusations."

Ellie squeezed her eyes shut. *Please, God...*

"I have been reluctant to cause harm to anyone. However, if you insist..." He feigned regret with his brows lowered, his voice soft and apologetic.

Vanna leaned toward Ellie, whispering, "If you want me to withdraw our request, I will."

Her throat tight, Ellie shook her head.

"I have been informed that an individual in Miss Vanna's employ," Robbins began, "has an employment history that includes working for an unsavory establishment."

Ellie gasped and her head snapped up. "That was years ago. It was an upscale restaurant, not unsavory at all," she muttered only loud enough for those nearby to hear.

"At one point," Robbins said, "that business was closed down due to a brawl resulting in several patrons being hospitalized."

"I wasn't even there that night," Ellie protested, her voice a hoarse whisper.

Robbins proceeded with a litany of her presumed immoral conduct, concluding, "Perhaps the most troubling evidence of this individual's inappropriate behavior is the fact that she consorted with a man of less than high moral standards and willingly admits she is an unwed mother."

A murmur of whispers spread around the council chambers like a prairie fire. Whether the audience agreed with Robbins or felt he had overstepped was impossible to tell.

Tears burning in her eyes, Ellie lowered her head. "I'll resign effective in the morning."

"You'll do no such thing," Vanna said. "You're not the only unwed mother in town."

"Don't do it," Arnie insisted. "There's no way Robbins can win this one."

Mayor Knudsen banged his gavel to silence the crowd. "Councilman Robbins has brought up some disturbing questions. However, his accusations do not *prove* actual misdeeds by the individual who he has yet to name."

The mayor looked to his fellow council members. "I believe we need to move slowly in this case. I'll entertain a motion to table the agenda item while further investigation is undertaken."

"Don't let him see you flinch," Arnie warned.

Her face as hot as if she were being burned at the stake, Ellie desperately tried to keep her chin up. When she'd read about the job opening at Ability Counts, she'd been so sure the Lord was leading her back home.

She touched the cross she wore. Would her credibility as a teacher now be totally destroyed in Potter Creek? And anywhere else she might go?

* * *

By the time the mayor adjourned the meeting, Arnie was steaming mad. He saw that Ellie's friends and fellow teachers were surrounding and supporting her. She'd be okay.

Arnie had something else he needed to do.

Spotting Amy Thurgood from the *Courier* across the room, he made his way through the departing crowd.

"Hey, Amy, I need a favor."

Her pencil stuck behind her ear, her glasses perched on top of her head, she smiled at Arnie. "Sure. What can I do for you?"

"Those accusations Robbins made tonight?"

"He was dropping a lot of bombshells there, if they're true."

"They're not," Arnie said. "Lies and distortions."

"How do you know that? He didn't name the individual involved."

"Ellie James."

The editor and sole reporter for the biweekly paper gaped at him. "You're kidding. She's a lovely young woman. I wouldn't think—"

"He asked her out, implying that if she agreed, he'd make sure the building permits would be approved. When she declined, he threatened her."

"Men! Some of them sure have their nerve." Amy plucked her notepad out of her shoulder bag and started to make notes. "Did you witness his threat?"

"No, but it's the truth." Flexing his hands, Arnie wished more than anything that he could personally make Robbins eat his words. Eight years ago, he would have gone after the sleazy character in a heartbeat. But no more. "He was talking about things that happened in Spokane while Ellie lived there and was going to college. I know you're a good enough investigative reporter to do a little fact-checking."

Her brows lifted. "I love it when a man tries to flatter me into doing something I want to do anyway."

He shook her hand. "Thanks, Amy. She deserves better than what Robbins is doing to her."

While Arnie couldn't protect Ellie's reputation with his fists, he figured—the good Lord willing—the power of the press could do the job just as well and not spill any blood.

Chapter Fourteen

"No, I will not accept your resignation." Vanna took the envelope Ellie had handed her, ripped it in half and dropped the pieces in the wastebasket beside her desk.

"After last night's council meeting, I've become a liability to the school," Ellie said reasonably, although the thought of leaving Ability Counts was breaking her heart. "If I'm no longer here, Robbins and the rest of the city council will have to—"

Vanna shook her head with such determination, her short gray hair quivered. "Jeffrey Robbins is all talk and no substance. By tabling our request, the mayor acted out of an abundance of caution. At next week's meeting everything will be sorted out. I promise."

Not as confident as her employer, Ellie started to object again. "But if the school loses the support of the community—"

"Here. This morning's *Courier.*" She held up the Wednesday edition of the paper. "There's barely a mention of Robbins's wild-eyed accusations last night. See for yourself."

Taking the paper, Ellie skimmed the report of the city council meeting. Only a brief mention of the school's building permit request being tabled appeared in the article. Nothing was said about the morals clause in the teachers' contracts.

Letting a sigh of relief escape, Ellie said, "If you're sure I'm not—"

"I'm absolutely positive." Vanna came around her desk and hugged Ellie. "You're a wonderful teacher. You take care of your students, and I'll take care of the politics for now."

As tall as Vanna was, and so slender she felt almost too bony, her hug and reassurance restored some measure of Ellie's confidence.

"If you change your mind about my resignation—"

"Hush. Go see to your children."

Ellie appreciated Vanna's loyalty and determination, but she wasn't entirely convinced it might not be better for her to resign and remove herself as a target of Robbins's ire.

Her spirits sank even deeper as she realized resigning would mean seeking another position. In all likelihood the new job wouldn't be in Potter Creek and would be a long way from Arnie. What chance would she have then to convince him of her feelings?

As the children began to arrive, one after another handed her a note from their mother or a small bouquet of chrysanthemums picked from their yard. In every case, the message supported Ellie and how much the children loved her. Obviously, the parents at the meeting had figured out Ellie had been the target of Robbins's attack.

Tears burned at the back of her eyes when Nancy, walking with her awkward gait, arrived in the classroom and handed Ellie a huge zucchini.

"We didn't have any flowers and my mommy didn't have time to make zucchini bread for you, so she said I could bring this instead."

Ellie knelt to hug and thank the child. "Tell your mother I love zucchini bread. Maybe I'll make some tonight to share with the whole class."

Nancy beamed. "I like walnuts in mine."

"So do I."

In that moment, Ellie realized, beyond being near Arnie, just how much she wanted to stay at Ability Counts. This was where she could best use her God-given talents. Working with children who had a physical disability and hearts that beat with so much love, they could teach the world the meaning of the Golden Rule. Do unto others as you would have them do unto you.

"Mommy, Arnie's van is in our driveway."

Ellie jumped to her feet, nearly knocking over her half-finished cup of coffee on the kitchen table. Relishing a lazy Saturday morning, she'd slept late and dressed in her grubby jeans and an old pullover sweater that had seen much better days. She didn't have a smidgen of makeup on, either.

Torie made a dash for the front door.

"Wait, honey. Let me see what he wants." Frowning, Ellie wondered at his midmorning visit. Could he be bringing bad news? Even so, she felt a flutter of anticipation in her midsection.

By the time she reached the front porch, Torie had already snared Sheila's attention, the two of them playing chase around the small front yard.

Arnie parked his wheelchair at the bottom of the steps. He was dressed in jeans and a pullover sweater that didn't look any more stylish than Ellie's.

"Hi." Slightly breathless, Ellie hesitated. "I didn't expect to see you this morning. Do you want to come inside?" She gestured vaguely toward the front door.

His lips twisted into a wry smile. "Not unless you've got a ramp hidden away. Those steps are going to be tough for me to climb."

Her cheeks heated with embarrassment. "Not exactly handicapped accessible, is it?" She walked down the steps and sat down on a lower step so she'd be at eye level with Arnie. The day was cool, with a few high-level clouds floating overhead. Rain was predicted for the mountains later in the day. "What's up?"

"I brought you this morning's *Courier*. Thought you'd like to see what Amy dug up." He tapped his finger on an article on the front page of the paper, below the fold. The headline read: Councilman's Accusations Unfounded.

Curious, and not a little concerned, Ellie took the newspaper. She scanned the article.

Councilman Jeffrey Robbins insinuated a teacher at Ability Counts...multiple violations of morals clause...facts obtained from witnesses...no suggestion of impropriety...impeccable references... question the councilman's motives...council should immediately approve...

Ellie looked up from the paper. "How did Amy decide to check out Robbins's story?"

Arnie lifted a single shoulder in an I-don't-have-a-clue-shrug.

She narrowed her gaze. "You talked to her, didn't you?"

"I might've mentioned something about slander and defamation of character. The reporting is all on Amy, though."

"Well, I sincerely thank you for whatever you did. She certainly did a great job." Leaning back, she rested her elbow on the step above her and smiled to herself. *Gotcha, Mr. Robbins.* "Now I'm extra glad I didn't agree to a date with Robbins."

"You were actually considering it?" Arnie asked, his voice rising. His expression darkened, and his brows lowered into a scowl.

As though her master had called her, Sheila came racing back to Arnie's side. Torie followed right behind the dog. She crumpled onto the ground beside Sheila, breathing hard from their game of chase.

"Not really, but I did start to wonder if it was worth it because it was the only way to get his vote. Potter Creek needs this school."

"Why didn't you trust me to take care of Robbins?" His grip on the armrests of his chair tightened.

"I had no idea you were going to get Amy to write an article to get me off the hook."

"You knew I didn't believe a word Robbins said. I wasn't going to let his insinuations stand if I could help it."

"Mommy, why are you and Arnie fighting?"

"We're not, honey," Ellie said. "We're having a little disagreement, is all."

"Then why are you shouting?" Torie asked.

"We're not." Arnie wheeled around and headed to his van.

"Wait, Arnie!" On her feet, Ellie hurried after him.

He activated the lift to lower it. "You can date anyone you want, Ellie. Like you said, it's no big deal."

"I don't have a date with anyone. I told Robbins no."

He rolled onto the lift and whipped around to glare at Ellie as Sheila hurried to join him. "I don't have any claim on you. Do whatever you want."

"But, Arnie—"

It was too late. He'd already wheeled inside and closed the door. Moments later the engine started. He backed the van and roared out the drive to the road, kicking up dust and pebbles.

Ellie's chin trembled. Tears she couldn't hold back crept down her cheeks. He didn't trust her. She'd broken that trust eight years ago. Now he was breaking her heart.

Arnie made it back to the ranch in record time.

The knot in his throat was so big, he could barely swallow. His head pounded as though there was an army of carpenters inside. His chest ached.

Ellie could date any guy she wanted to.

So what's been keeping you from asking her out?

She wouldn't want to go out with me. She proved that when she bailed out of Potter Creek years ago.

She came back, didn't she?

She didn't come back for me. She came for the job.

Which happens to deal with handicapped children. What does that prove?

Maybe she's changed. Maybe loving someone who has a disability doesn't bother her anymore.

Shaking his head to dislodge the irritating voice that had invaded his thoughts, Arnie parked the van between two pickup trucks by his new house. The construction crew was installing windows today, anxious to get the place sealed up before winter storms arrived. The interior work could be done at a more leisurely pace.

Arnie hoped to be moved in by December, before Mindy's baby arrived. Not that he didn't like babies. He just wanted to give his brother and his wife some privacy. There would be plenty of time for him to play Uncle Arnie with the kid.

He rolled up the ramp into the house. Sheila's toe-nails tapped a rapid beat on the flooring right behind him.

"How's it going?" he asked Tim, who was installing the big picture window in its frame in the living room. Scott Derringer was helping from the outside.

Tim grunted. "If we don't drop this sucker, I'd say we're doing fine." He jammed a sliver of wood between the window and the frame to keep it straight.

Arnie glanced around, checking on the crew's progress. The kitchen windows were in place, and Daniel was installing insulation around the frames to keep out drafts. Arnie had installed wallboard as high as he could reach in all the rooms except the spare bedroom. He'd go work on that now.

Maybe pounding in a few nails would improve his mood.

By late afternoon, his buddies had packed up their tools, ready to head home.

Arnie followed them out. "Thanks, guys. Really appreciate your help."

They waved off his thanks as they piled into their pickups.

The last to leave, Tim slung his tool belt over his shoulder. "You going to the church picnic tomorrow?"

"Yeah, I guess." He'd forgotten about the annual picnic. There were lots of games for the kids, and the guys usually put together a game of flag football. Since he wasn't exactly mobile on a grass field, he was the designated quarterback. Occasionally overeager, the opposing players had managed to tackle him only a couple of times. No harm done.

"Great. I'll see you at church, then." Tim sauntered down to his truck, put his tools in the lockbox in the back and drove away.

Watching him leave, Arnie felt a sinking feeling. Chances were good Ellie would bring Torie to the picnic.

With a big crowd in attendance and decent luck, he'd be able to avoid her. He wouldn't have to apologize for being so stupid at the thought of her dating other men. He hoped.

Chapter Fifteen

Ellie drove her car out of the church parking lot to join the caravan of vehicles headed for Riverside Park and the church picnic. Although there were still rain clouds hovering above the mountain peaks of the Rockies to the west, overhead the sky was clear and the air crisp with a hint of Halloween on the way. A perfect day for hot chocolate and toasting marshmallows over an open fire.

With her mother sitting next to her, and Torie in the backseat, memories of the last time she'd visited Riverside Park swept over Ellie. She could almost feel the late-summer sun on her face, the icy-cold river water.

A half dozen couples were playing six-way keep-away with a Frisbee in a clearing near the river. The breeze, and the unpredictability of the flying saucer, resulted in more than one player having to chase the Frisbee into the water, which wasn't too deep that summer.

Arnie was the tallest among the boys and the best

thrower. Regretfully, Ellie couldn't get the hang of the thing, which meant Arnie ended up in the creek. A lot. To the great rejoicing and raucous laughter of his buddies.

After his third dunking, they changed their position so she was throwing *away* from the water. But this time Arnie's effort went sailing over Ellie's head. His brother Daniel raced to intercept it.

"No!" she cried, stumbling backward to catch the Frisbee.

"Watch out!" Arnie shouted.

Daniel splashed into the water to snare the Frisbee. "You lose, bro!"

The slippery rocks and uneven footing made Ellie lose her balance. She fell backward. Gooseflesh shivered across her body as she slid under the surface. She swallowed a mouthful of water.

The next thing she knew, Arnie was pulling her up out of the freezing water, laughing at her. Her hair hung like a wet mop, dripping. He looked at her with such amazing love in his eyes that she shivered.

Lowering his head to hers, he soundly kissed her.

When he broke the kiss, he spoke in a voice rough with emotion. "We'll get 'em next time, Ellie. Nobody can beat us. We belong together."

We belong together. She still remembered his words. The joy she'd felt in her heart. The future she'd anticipated. She'd been so young, so sure nothing would change.

How could she have been so wrong?

Following the car in front of her, Ellie turned into the park entrance and drove over a bridge that spanned the river. The water looked higher than usual for this time of year, white waves splashing over the rocks lining the riverbed, carrying debris from upstream down toward the much larger Jefferson River.

"Is Arnie going to be at the picnic?" Torie asked from the backseat.

Ellie's heart squeezed an anxious beat, and she glanced in the rearview mirror at her daughter. "I don't know. I guess we'll see when we get there. I do know there will be lots of games for you to play and some of your friends from Sunday school will be there."

Dozens of cars and pickups were already parked at the group picnic area. The ladies who had organized the event had spread tablecloths on the sturdy picnic tables, and a handful of men were laying a fire in the stone ring. Nearby, children had claimed a turn on the swings and the merry-go-round.

Ellie pulled into a parking place. Her mother, who had been quiet the whole way, and Torie got out of the car.

"Can I go play on the swings?" Torie asked.

"Go ahead. But we'll be eating soon. Mom, you go on and help the ladies. I'll bring the ice chest."

Ellie opened her door just as Arnie's van drove into the handicapped slot next to her. She swallowed hard. She didn't want him to think she'd intentionally picked this spot next to the handicapped slot.

Within moments, the van door opened and the lift lowered Arnie and Sheila to the ground.

"So here we are," Arnie said, "visiting the scenes of our youth."

"We had lots of good times here."

His guarded perusal of her brought heat to her face again, and she knew he was remembering warm summer nights and the kisses they had shared. Kisses she had relished, memories she had left behind when she moved to Spokane.

"Why did you tell me to go away?" Her words were a whispered plea for understanding.

Wrinkles scored his forehead. "I don't remember telling you that."

"You did." The pain of rejection still had the power to bring her to her knees. "You told me two times to leave and not to bother to come back. The first time I figured you were still fuzzy from the meds. The second time…" She'd fled the room, crying. Nearly hysterical. The worst day of her life. How could he not remember when his words had been etched in her memory by the acid of betrayal?

He rubbed his forehead as though trying to recreate the moment. "I'm sorry, Ellie. I really don't remember. I was pretty much out of it for a long time. But I do recall thinking later on that you were smart to get on with your life without me."

In order to protect herself, to keep on going, she'd tried to believe that was true. She'd never been able to fully convince herself. Instead, she'd carried the guilt of leaving him for eight long years.

"I guess you still don't want me in your life," she said.

He wiped his hand across his face. "Nothing has changed, has it? I'm stuck in this chair for the rest of my life."

And Ellie was stuck loving him.

Turning away, she opened the back door of her car and pulled out the ice chest. "I need to get this over to the tables. We'll be eating soon." She walked quickly away so he wouldn't see the tears that burned in her eyes. Her love was pointless if he saw himself only as a man in a wheelchair who was unable to love her in return.

"Ellie!"

She turned at the sound of her name and found Mindy hurrying toward her, her advancing pregnancy giving her a distinctive waddle.

"Hey, Mindy. Looks like your pregnancy is progressing nicely," she said with a grin.

"Nicely, if you think looking like an elephant is in style this season."

Ellie laughed. "Your glow makes up for everything else. You look wonderful."

They visited for a few minutes, then Pastor Redmond called everyone together to say grace before they ate.

Too excited to eat, Torie managed only a few bites before she was off again to play with her friends.

Ellie lingered over her lunch, indulging in a magnificent five-layer chocolate cake for dessert. She'd worry about her diet tomorrow.

Most of the men had divided themselves into two teams to play football in an open, grassy area.

Squinting, Ellie gaped at the players. It couldn't be.

"Mindy, is that Arnie playing quarterback?" *In his wheelchair?* Was there anything that man *couldn't* do? How could he possibly think of himself as disabled?

"Sure is. Daniel says his brother is dead-on with his passes. His team wins every year. Of course, they have a rule that no one can rush the passer."

"I should think not." If they did, they'd probably squash Arnie and trample poor Sheila, who doggedly stayed near her master.

"Speaking of Arnie," Mindy said. "How's it going with the two of you?"

Ellie shook her head. "At the moment, it's not going anywhere and probably won't." To her dismay.

"I'm sorry to hear—"

A piercing scream penetrated the bucolic scene.

Everyone froze right where they were as if a snapshot had been taken. Only the breeze in the trees and the rushing water broke the silence.

Automatically, Ellie looked around to find Torie. A few minutes ago she'd been playing hide-and-seek with some of her friends. But now Ellie couldn't see her. An icy shiver of fear slid down her spine.

"Mom...my!"

The blood-chilling scream propelled Ellie to her feet.

Victoria! Recognizing her child's cry, she raced toward the water.

Vaguely, she was aware of others running with her, but her entire focus was on reaching her child. Her baby girl. What had happened? Where was Torie? Why hadn't she kept better track of her daughter?

"Torie!" she shouted. "Where are you?"

Her heart pounding, she reached the edge of the creek, but Torie wasn't in sight. She looked up and down the fast-moving water, which seemed to be roiling even more violently than before.

"There!" someone shouted.

Her gaze shifted to follow the direction in which a woman was pointing. There she saw her daughter's dark red hair bobbing above the roiling water. *Please, Lord, help her….*

Suddenly there was scrambling downstream. Apparently while others had headed toward where Torie had fallen into the river, Arnie and some of the men had angled downstream to intercept her. In his wheelchair, Arnie was perched on an outcropping of rock above the creek. He leaned forward. Waiting.

With his powerful arms, he launched himself forward into the creek only feet in front of a frantically crying, splashing Torie.

Ellie's heart stopped. No way could Arnie swim without the use of his legs. Not in this rapidly churning water. They'd both be killed. Drowned.

Breaking into a run, she dashed toward the spot where Arnie had entered the water. Brush whipped at her legs. Branches snatched at her face. She couldn't lose both of them. Not the two people on earth whom she loved more than life itself.

Yelling at his brother, Daniel leaped into the water, swimming after Arnie. Other men followed the path along the creek, ready to go in the water, as well.

Arnie's head appeared above the water. He spun around. Spotted Torie. With massive strokes of his arms, he swam after her. He bounced off a boulder. Just ahead of him, Torie became lodged momentarily between the rocks. Then the power of the rain-swollen river swept her downstream again.

Arnie didn't give up. He pursued Torie with the strength of an Olympic athlete.

Torie became lodged between other rocks. Ellie could see blood oozing from her daughter's forehead. She lay lax in the water, a rag doll, limbs akimbo, no longer fighting the pull of the stream.

Sheila, who'd been trailing along beside the creek, jumped in to aid her master just as Arnie reached Torie. He wrapped an arm around the child and held on to a rock to prevent them both from careening downstream, where a waterfall dropped into a steep canyon.

Daniel caught up with the pair, wrapping his arms around both of them.

Ellie prayed for their safety. All three of them.

Sheila paddled valiantly toward Arnie. The current swept the dog past her goal. She turned, fighting her way back against the force of the creek.

Slowly she inched toward Arnie, only to be driven back again by the powerful surge of water.

Covering her mouth with her hands to prevent a scream, Ellie held her breath.

Finally, Sheila reached an eddy near Arnie, the water smoother, and paddled closer to her master.

When the dog was within arm's reach, Arnie risked his hold on the rock and grabbed on to Sheila, looping his arm around her neck. Daniel latched onto Torie. Together they all swam for shore. Sheila's head dipped below the waves time and time again. Arnie's face contorted with pain. His black hair matted against his head. Daniel kept Torie above water as he stroked toward those waiting to help.

When they reached the shallows along the creek side, a half dozen men waded into the water to help Arnie. Daniel lifted Torie in his arms and staggered out of the creek. Her arms and legs limp, the child showed no sign of life.

All Ellie could do was drop to her knees beside her child as Daniel rolled Torie over and drove the water from Torie's lungs. Turning her onto her back, Daniel held the child's nose closed and began breathing into Torie's mouth.

Ellie prayed as she never had before.

Chapter Sixteen

❧

Torie coughed up some water and moaned.

Ellie nearly collapsed in relief.

"There you go, sweetheart." Daniel rocked back on his heels and looked up at Ellie. The relief in his dark eyes reflected her own.

"Thank you," she whispered, kneeling beside her child and taking Torie's hand. She squeezed it gently. "You're okay, baby. You're okay now."

Torie coughed again but didn't open her eyes. The gash on her head created a river of blood that slid past her hairline. A purple bruise colored her cheek. Ellie couldn't tell if there were any bones broken.

Ellie's stomach nearly rebelled at the possibility.

"Wake up, sweetie. Mommy wants to see your eyes."

Ellie's mother squatted down beside her. "Is she all right?" Her whisper-thin voice trembled.

"I don't know," Ellie answered.

She dug in the pocket of her slacks for something to

staunch the flow of blood. Daniel handed her a clean handkerchief. She pressed it to Torie's wound.

"I'm going to go check on Arnie," he said.

Keeping the pressure on Torie's wound, Ellie looked around for Arnie. He was still on the ground near the riverbank, several concerned-looking men hovering around him.

Her heart stilled and filled with so much love she thought it might burst. Without Arnie, she could have lost her child. He'd been the first to reach Torie. He'd saved her life, risking his own in the process, holding her out of the water until more help could arrive. *Please let him be all right, Lord.*

Apparently, someone had called 9-1-1. A yellow and white fire rescue truck roared into the picnic grounds, siren wailing. The truck pulled to a stop and the driver cut the siren, but the red lights continued to circle above the truck cab like the flashing eyes of a dragon. Ellie shivered.

The two paramedics separated, one running toward Arnie and the other to Torie.

A young man in a firefighter uniform knelt beside Torie and placed his stethoscope on her tiny chest. He listened for only a moment, then began gently examining the child, searching for injuries.

"What happened here, ma'am?"

"She fell in the water. That man on the ground over there saved her." Arnie O'Brien, her hero.

He glanced in Arnie's direction. "Good man."

"The best," she said with heartfelt emphasis.

"Mommy…"

Thank you, Lord! "I'm right here, sweetie. This nice man is going to make sure you're all right."

"Grandma BarBar's here, too, honey." Barbara's voice hitched. "You're going to be fine. Try not to move. Just let the nice man do his job."

The paramedic sat back on his haunches. "She's probably got a concussion. Some bruising and contusions, but no breaks that I can tell. I'm going to get a gurney and strap her down nice and tight just in case she's got back or neck problems. We'll take her to the hospital and let the docs take a look."

"May I ride with her?" Ellie asked, a plea in her voice.

"Sure. Glad to have you along." With a smile, he patted Torie's cheek. "You stay right here, princess. I'm coming right back, and I'm going to give you a ride in my chariot."

"Okay." She gave him a weak smile.

Ellie handed her mother the car keys. "Can you drive yourself home?"

"Nonsense. I'll meet you at the hospital."

A smile of gratitude lifted Ellie's lips. She didn't want to sit for hours in a hospital waiting room alone while doctors did who knew what to her daughter. Ellie needed her mother's steadying hand.

"Thanks, Mom." She hadn't seen her mother look so determined, so sure of herself in years. Because of her love for her grandchild, Barbara had risen to the occasion. Ellie would have to remember that and trust her mother had the strength to endure whatever came her way.

It took several minutes for the two paramedics to load both Arnie and Torie in their vehicle. One paramedic stayed in the back with his patients, and Ellie squeezed in between Torie and Arnie.

Daniel had to hold on to Sheila to prevent the wet, muddy dog from jumping up to be with Arnie.

"I'll see you at the hospital," Daniel said as the driver closed the door to the vehicle.

"How are you doing?" Ellie asked Arnie. His wet flannel shirt clung to his chest. The paramedic had covered him with a warm blanket, as he had Torie.

"I'm good. Couple of cracked ribs, maybe. I'll live."

She took his hand and squeezed his fingers. "I don't know how to thank you."

"Don't, Ellie." His expression unreadable, he looked away and removed his hand from hers. "Don't thank me."

"You saved my daughter's life." Her voice rose, challenging his statement. "You could've been killed yourself," she protested, stunned and hurt by his withdrawal.

His jaw muscle flexed. "If I had two good legs, she wouldn't have gotten so banged up."

The rescue vehicle lurched forward. Ellie held on to a safety railing.

"What are you talking about?" she asked. "You jumped in the river first. You were the first one to reach her."

"I couldn't let her drown." He turned back to her, his eyes bleak. "I didn't want you to lose her."

Ellie's heart expanded with love and admiration. The man didn't seem to realize that what he'd done was heroic. And he'd done it for her and her daughter.

Not caring that the paramedic was there, Ellie leaned forward and pressed a kiss to Arnie's lips, tasted the chilly water. It hurt that he didn't respond, but she was past the point of caring.

"Arnie O'Brien, you can't stop me from thanking you, and you can't stop me from loving you. That's just the way it is."

He scrolled his brows into a frown. "You stopped loving me a long time ago."

"No, I didn't stop loving you. I chickened out, I admit. I couldn't stay in Potter Creek after you told me to go away. I was young and foolish. I shouldn't have believed you. But I'm back now. And I'm here to stay."

Siren wailing, the truck bounced in a pothole, then rode up onto the highway.

Arnie grimaced. "Torie needs a man around who can climb trees with her, teach her to play soccer. A man with two good legs. You need a man who can love you in every way you have a right to be loved."

"And you can't love me at all." That wasn't a question, but a statement of fact. Ellie pressed her lips together.

He turned his face to the wall again. "I didn't say that."

His voice was so low, and the siren so loud, Ellie didn't think she'd heard him clearly. "What did you say?"

"Nothing. It doesn't matter."

Ellie thought it did matter. Wanting to drag the words out of him again, she fisted her hands.

"Mommy, I don't like this chariot." Blood had oozed through the gauze bandage the paramedic had wrapped around her forehead, turning it red.

Stroking Torie's head and brushing her damp hair away from her forehead, Ellie said, "It's okay, sweetie. It won't be a long ride." She glanced at the medic.

"Thirty minutes," he silently mouthed.

Ellie grimaced. Thirty minutes would seem like an eternity to Torie. In this sparsely populated part of Montana, hospitals were few and far between.

"Hey, squirt," Arnie said to Torie. "How're you doing?"

"My head hurts."

"Yeah, mine does, too. Next time we go swimming, let's pick a spot that doesn't have so many rocks."

"I don't want to go swimming anymore." Tears bloomed in Torie's eyes. Ellie wiped them away with a tissue.

"Okay. Where do you want to go?" Arnie asked.

"I want to go home!" Her tiny voice wobbled.

"How 'bout the zoo?" Arnie asked. "I really like to watch the monkeys climb around in their cage. What do you think? We could have a lot of fun at the zoo."

"I like giraffes."

"Terrific. We'll see the monkeys and the giraffes. What else?"

Ellie knew Arnie was trying to keep Torie's mind off her injuries and the swaying ride of the emergency vehicle. She blessed him for his thoughtfulness.

If only she hadn't been a coward about his injuries eight years ago, they'd be married by now. He'd be the father of her children.

But that would mean she wouldn't have had Torie. For that reason alone, she'd never want to erase the past. It was what it was.

She could only pray Arnie could find a way to trust her again, open his heart to her love and know that she would always be faithful to him.

At long last, the ambulance pulled up to the hospital emergency entrance. The back doors popped open.

"What have we got here, Walt?" a nurse in light blue scrubs asked.

"Female child with a possible concussion and adult male with broken ribs," the medic replied. "Both patients are stable."

"Good enough. Let's get them out of there."

"Chariot ride is over, Torie." Squeezing her daughter's hand, Ellie eased out of the ambulance. She stood by while the medics retrieved the gurneys.

The nurse said, "Looks like your husband and daughter have had a busy afternoon."

"An unplanned dip in the river." Ellie didn't correct the nurse's assumption that Arnie was her husband. It took too much effort to deny what should have been and never would be.

Arnie didn't make eye contact as an orderly rolled him though the yawning doors to the emergency room.

Aching and heavyhearted, Ellie held Torie's hand as she was wheeled through the same doors.

Help me, Lord. Help me to let go if there's no hope.

"That was a pretty dumb thing you did, bro."

Arnie opened one eye to peer up at his brother from his hospital bed. Doctors had pinched, poked and jabbed him in the emergency room, x-rayed and wrapped his broken ribs. Finally they decided to keep him overnight for observation.

He hated hospitals. The smell of antiseptic. The rattle of food and laundry carts, the wheels squeaking and rumbling down the hallway, unseen. The bark of the loudspeaker paging a doctor—stat. Drafty hospital gowns.

It was the craziest stunt he'd ever pulled. What crazy impulse had made him, a paraplegic, think he could swim in a rain-swollen creek well enough to save himself, much less a helpless child?

"Everybody's calling you a hero."

"I was stupid." Just about as stupid as wanting to believe Ellie, wanting her to kiss him again, wanting to take her at her word that she'd never stopped loving him. Now that was *really* stupid.

He still wasn't the right man for Ellie. She and her daughter deserved so much more.

Daniel lowered the guardrail and sat on the edge of the bed. "I checked on Torie. The docs stitched her head up and sent her home. Ellie's supposed to keep her eye on her and wake her every couple of hours during the night."

"She's going to be okay, then?"

"The docs think so, or they wouldn't have sent her home."

Closing his eyes, Arnie said a prayer of thanksgiving. "What'd you do with Sheila?"

"Outside with Mindy. I've gotta get her to a vet for a checkup and a bath before the hospital will let her come up here with you. I put your chair here next to your bed if you need it."

"Thanks for taking care of everything."

"No problem." Daniel gripped his brother's hand in an arm wrestling hold, the way they had when they were kids, but he didn't take advantage of Arnie's weakened state. Not this time. "You get some rest. I'll come back in the morning to bail you out of this place."

"Come early. I don't want to stay here any longer than I have to."

After Daniel left, Arnie lay on his back, staring at the acoustical tile ceiling. If he had the energy, he could count the holes in each tile.

But what would be the point?

He was stuck here in the bed like a turtle rolled onto its back. Useless. Unable to escape. Any movement as painful as though somebody was stabbing him in the ribs with a sharp stick.

He curled his hands into fists.

It was just as well Ellie hadn't come upstairs to tell him she was taking Torie home. She didn't need to see him like this. Not again.

Not like he'd been when she'd left him eight years ago.

Ellie held herself together that evening until after dinner, when she put Torie to bed and was sure her child was sleeping peacefully. She continued to sit beside Torie, watching her breathe, the pink princess quilt gently rising and falling, and let the tears roll.

She'd been so scared!

Her lungs seized, and she reached for a tissue to blow her nose. What if Arnie hadn't been there? What if she'd lost Torie?

"Ellie." Standing in the doorway, her mother spoke softly. "Come on, dear. She'll be fine now. Come sit with me in the living room."

"I don't want to leave—"

Barbara held out her hand. "You don't want her to wake and see you crying."

Her mother was right, of course. But it was hard to leave Torie. To walk out of the room and not check her every breath. To not want to hold on to her all through the night.

Ellie stepped to the doorway. Her mother looped her arm around Ellie's waist, and they walked together down the hallway to the living room. Barbara sat down beside her on the couch.

"God was watching over us today." Barbara patted Ellie's hands, which had nearly shredded the tissue.

"God and Arnie," she said.

"Yes, and Arnie, too." She leaned back on the couch and sighed deeply. "I believe I seriously misjudged that young man. Years ago, when you were seeing him, I liked him well enough, but I was afraid for you. I wanted more than an early marriage followed by babies for you. I wanted you to have an education, something I never had a chance to get."

Ellie slid her mother a surprised look. She'd had no idea Barbara had even considered going to college. She'd never said a word. She'd seemed content being a potato farmer's wife.

"After Arnie's accident," Barbara said, "I knew if you stayed, you'd marry him and that would mean you'd never have the opportunities you deserved. So I encouraged you to leave. It nearly broke my heart. Your father's, too."

This was definitely news to Ellie. She'd believed the whole reason Barbara had insisted she move to Spokane was to prevent her from marrying a paraplegic and being tied down as her family had been with Uncle Bob.

"Then you came back home, and I was afraid you were going to take up with Arnie again."

"He doesn't want me, Mother."

"I'm not so sure of that." She brushed Ellie's hair back from her temple, much like Ellie had done with Torie's hair. "At Torie's birthday party, he was wonderful with the children. And I saw him looking at you. I know when a man is in love. I saw that same look in your father's eyes every day of our life together. With you and Arnie, it rather frightened me, I admit. I still didn't want you two to get together."

"Well, you're going to get your way. First, Arnie can't bring himself to trust me, because I left him before. And second, perhaps more importantly, I don't think he believes he's enough of a man for any woman."

"After what he did today?" Barbara snorted. "A man who has that much courage and gumption, who's that willing to risk his own life, is a man any woman would be happy to marry."

"I'm glad to hear you say that, Mother, but you don't have to convince me. It's what Arnie believes that's holding him back." There was nothing Ellie could do to change his mind.

Pensive, Barbara rubbed her fingertip over the slight cleft in her chin, a mannerism that spoke of deep thought. "Arnie has been quite active in church these past few years. The Lord has always been good about working through Pastor Redmond. Maybe you should ask him to talk to Arnie."

Ellie was more than willing to talk to the pastor about Arnie. She loved Arnie so much that she'd use the biggest megaphone she could find to get someone to wake him to what they were both missing. The love they had to share.

But would Arnie listen to the pastor?

Maybe she'd talk to him after the city council settled the Ability Counts issue....

Chapter Seventeen

Two days later, shortly after the city council meeting had been called to order, a cheer went up from the packed chamber. They'd won!

The city council had approved the building permit for Ability Counts.

As though lifted by the enthusiasm of the crowd, Ellie jumped to her feet. She embraced Vanna, her arms easily encompassing the slender woman.

"You did it!" Ellie said over the applause and cheers.

"We did it together. All of us." Her voice breathless, her eyes damp with tears, Vanna returned her embrace. Her emotions were so powerful, she trembled. Ellie recalled how pale and tired Vanna had seemed all day and then again when she arrived at the city council meeting. She'd been rubbing her left arm and jaw almost constantly. The stress of the past few weeks had obviously taken its toll, Ellie concluded.

Everyone who was involved with the school had

turned out for the Tuesday night meeting. Everyone except Jeffrey Robbins, who had suddenly taken ill, according to the mayor.

Smiling a gotcha grin, and tickled way down to her toes, Ellie chided herself for not being concerned for Jeffrey's health. Whatever *illness* had kept him from the meeting, he'd brought on himself. And the Chronicle had put the facts in print.

Supporters gathered around Vanna, congratulating her, shaking her hand and giving her more hugs. Between hugs and good wishes, she rubbed her jaw and shifted her shoulders, as though trying to relax tense muscles. Understandable, given the situation and the weeks of preparation and planning for this night.

Ellie slipped past her, taking time to high-five her fellow teachers and thank some of her students' parents before she reached Arnie, who was sitting at the end of the aisle. She walked up beside him.

"I owe you another big thank-you." Ellie hadn't talked to him since the ride in the ambulance from the picnic and didn't know quite what to expect from him. Nor had she had a chance to speak to Pastor Redmond as yet. "If you hadn't sicced Amy at the *Courier* on Robbins, the outcome might've been different."

He shrugged, wincing a little, as though his ribs still bothered him. They probably would for another few weeks. "I figured I had to do something. The school means a lot to Vanna."

"To me, too."

"I know. It's the reason you came back to Potter Creek."

"True. But now there's another reason I'm glad I came back."

He gave her a sideways scowl. "Another reason?"

Was every man as dense as Arnie? She pressed in on his personal space. "Maybe, after all this time, I'm hoping we might have another chance."

"You want a second chance? For us?"

"Does that seem so strange to you?" Her chest constricted with a mix of love and fear of loss. *Please God, let him see how much I love him.*

Straightening, she rested her hand on his shoulder, the breadth of his muscular upper body stretching his sweater, revealing his elemental strength beneath the fabric. She could feel his heat seeping through the cashmere to warm her palm. And her heart.

If anything, Arnie's expression was more confused than ever.

The mayor banged his gavel. "Ladies and gentlemen," he shouted over the crowd noise. "We have some more business to conduct. If those of you who aren't concerned with the next agenda item could step outside, we'd appreciate it."

Most of the crowd began to shuffle toward the exits. Ellie fell in step beside Arnie, her hand still on his shoulder as they moved slowly toward the rear of the chambers. Sheila walked beside him on the opposite side.

Outside, in a patio lined by willow trees starting to

shed their golden leaves, the throng of Ability Counts supporters continued to chat among themselves, all smiles.

Daniel and Mindy, who'd been sitting in the back of the meeting room, made their way to Arnie and Ellie.

"Hey, you two." Daniel aimed a knowing look at Ellie and her hand resting on Arnie's shoulder. "You two are looking pretty proud of yourselves after your big win."

"You'd better believe it, bro."

With heat flooding her face, Ellie dropped her hand to her side. "Vanna's very pleased about getting the permit. It's been a long road for her. Now all she has to do is raise ten gazillion dollars to actually build the new classrooms."

"She's a master at fundraising," Arnie commented.

"Better her than me," Ellie said. "I'm happy simply teaching my kids and watching them grow."

Tilting his head up, Arnie slanted her a look she couldn't read, somehow both serious and curious. "I'm guessing you're quite capable of doing anything you set your mind to, including fundraising."

She laughed off his comment. "I, for one, hope Ability Counts doesn't have to test your supposition."

"Oh, I don't know. You can be very persuasive."

Lifting her brows, Ellie wondered if Arnie meant that as a compliment. Or was he simply flattering her? Or maybe, she prayed, he'd finally gotten the message: she loved him.

From the middle of the crowd a man shouted, "We need a doctor over here."

"Somebody call nine-one-one!"

"I don't think she's breathing."

For an instant, no one moved. Then, in tandem, Daniel and Arnie shot toward the center of the patio, plowing their way through the immobile crowd.

Instinctively, Mindy placed her hand over her distended belly. "What do you think happened?"

Remembering the sight of Daniel hauling Torie out of the water, Ellie shivered. "Whatever it is, it doesn't sound good."

Whispered words sped through the onlookers like a dam had sprung a leak. The murmur spread, widening its wake, creating waves of gasps and soulful prayers, until the words reached Ellie's ears.

Vanna. Collapsed. Unconscious. Heart attack!

Dread thrummed in Ellie's chest. Tears stung her eyes. She covered her mouth to hold back a sob. Her fear was colored with desperation; her panic smothered in denial.

She'd just been talking with Vanna, applauding her success. She had sat beside her during the entire meeting. She'd been fine. Perhaps a little pale, her face had had a sheen of sweat, but Ellie had credited that to the importance of getting the permits. The strain Vanna had been under. And the excitement that followed.

She'd never considered Vanna might be ill.

As though drawn by the slender thread of hope, she eased her way through the crowd until she reached

Arnie. He took her hand, squeezing her fingers as they watched Daniel press rhythmically on Vanna's chest.

The crowd remained silent, respectful, prayerful as Daniel counted, "One. Two. Three…"

"Where's the ambulance? The rescue squad?" Ellie whispered.

Arnie shook his head. "They'll be here soon." The concern in his voice matched her own.

The county fire department and police department served Potter Creek. The closest fire station was ten miles away. The response time was slower than the community would like, but a lack of funds…

Feeling helpless, heartsick and useless, she clung to Arnie's hand. *Vanna, her boss. Her mentor. Her friend.*

Minutes passed, until she finally heard the siren approaching. While she waited, she mentally reviewed the way Vanna had been acting. Had the frequent rubbing of her arm, and then her jaw, been a symptom of something more than simply stress? Had Vanna been on the verge of a heart attack for weeks? Or longer?

The crowd parted. Two paramedics dashed across the patio and knelt beside Vanna.

Ellie prayed they had arrived in time.

Two hours later, more than a dozen people waited in the hospital lobby outside the emergency room entrance. Some stood and paced. Others sat in uncomfortable plastic chairs, huddled with their friends, talking quietly among themselves. No one bothered with the array of magazines or hospital pamphlets available to while away their time. Their combined distress and concern for Vanna made even the air in the room feel heavy, as though an approaching storm threatened to overwhelm them.

Among those who had gathered for the vigil were Pastor Redmond, several of Ellie's fellow teachers, two sets of parents and a few of Vanna's friends who had known and loved her for years.

Mindy and Daniel had gone back to the ranch. Rather than drive herself to the hospital, after letting her mother know she'd be late, Ellie had ridden with Arnie, grateful to have his company and his calming strength.

Except her calm had worn off after the first hour of waiting.

"If the worst happens," she asked, "what will become of Ability Counts?"

"The school will go on as it has been. Vanna created a solid foundation for her dream. The school is more than a single person, which is what she wanted. It's parents and teachers, supporters from all across the state, and the children themselves. In the worst case, the board would have to hire a new director, of course."

Ellie wondered how the board could possibly find anyone as devoted to the school's mission as Vanna was.

Instantly, she halted that thought. Vanna wasn't going to die. She'd be fine. People survived heart attacks every day. Vanna would be no exception. She might have to stay off work for a time, or perhaps work fewer hours. But with rest and rehabilitation, she'd recover. She had to!

The door to the E.R. swung open. Everyone turned as a woman in blue scrubs hurried out and turned down a hallway. She didn't spare so much as a glance toward those waiting in the lobby.

Unable to sit still any longer, Ellie popped to her feet. "What's taking them so long? Why doesn't someone come tell us what's going on?"

"Easy, El." Arnie snared her hand and rubbed his thumb over her knuckles. "They're doing everything they can for Vanna. We just have to wait it out."

"Wait. And pray."

"True." He glanced around. "There's a chapel down the hall. Let's go check it out."

"But if someone comes out—"

"They'll let us know." Giving her hand a tug, he wheeled around, heading for the chapel. Sheila fell into step right beside him.

Ellie had little choice but to follow.

Soft music, a string quartet, was piped into the dimly lit room. On a background of pastel green, murals of the Rockies, pine forests and prairies decorated the walls. A water feature at the front of the chapel showed a stream spilling out of the wall to cascade down a mountainside, splashing into a natural pool.

The serenity of the room, the peace and God's presence washed over Ellie as she sat down on a wooden pew. Her shoulders relaxed. Her worried frown eased. Breathing deeply, she caught the scent of pine in the air, heard the rushing water and felt the cool mountain breeze on her overheated cheeks.

Arnie was right. Prayer was the answer.

As though he'd read her mind, he took her hand and bowed his head. She leaned forward to the back of the next pew and rested her head on her hand.

"Dear Heavenly Father," Arnie began in a quiet yet deeply resonant baritone. "We are here to plead for Your help for our friend Vanna Coulter. We know she is Your devoted servant and that You have the power to see her through this crisis. We ask that You heal her and bring her back to us so that she can continue serving You and complete the work which has been her life-long calling."

Tears crept down Ellie's cheeks as Arnie prayed, his voice steady, his words coming from the heart.

He finished the prayer with "Thy will be done. Amen."

"Amen," she echoed with a sob and turned to him, putting her head on his shoulder, her cheek caressed by his cashmere sweater. It was the most natural thing in the world to have his arms around her. He held her, patted her back and brushed tiny kisses to her hair and forehead, murmuring sweet words of comfort.

When she lifted her head, his shirt was soaked and there were tears in his eyes.

She looked up to find Pastor Redmond standing in the chapel doorway. Lines of grief etched his face, making him look suddenly old and tired.

"She's with the Lord now." His solemn pronouncement rang hollow in the muted silence of the chapel. "She's sitting at His right hand, watching over us."

Sorrow clogged Ellie's chest until she could barely draw a breath.

"She would want us to continue her work," the pastor said. "The teachers and parents have asked that you come join them. They look up to you, Ellie, and need you."

Ellie swiped her eyes with the back of her hand. What could she possibly do to help them when her own grief was so fresh, so raw, weighing on her as though a mountain avalanche had buried her?

"Go, Ellie," Arnie said. "Be strong for them."

She studied him, the sorrow in his dark eyes as deep as her own. "I need you with me."

He responded with a solemn nod.

Arnie followed Ellie and the pastor back to the lobby, awed by the way she had set her own grief aside. Her back straight, her head held high, she approached her fellow teachers and Vanna's friends. To each she offered a hug and whispered words of encouragement.

"How will we tell the children?" Dawn asked, her voice unsteady, her eyes red-rimmed.

"We'll tell them the truth," Ellie answered. "The Lord called Vanna to His side. Her work here on earth is done. We'll all miss her. To honor her memory, we'll carry on with what she started. That's what she would want us to do."

"But how?" Marlene asked. "Vanna was the one with

the vision. She was at the center of Ability Counts. The core of it."

"She shared her vision. It's inside each of us." Ellie tapped her chest, over her heart, as she glanced around at the somber group. "That was Vanna's gift. Together we'll bring that vision to fruition."

The tightness of loss and grief in Arnie's chest eased, replaced with the hope and confidence Ellie imparted to the others. The fact that she was years younger than many of those she hugged and encouraged didn't matter. Somehow they sensed that she was a leader, someone to lean on.

She was not the same young woman who had deserted him so many years ago. The changes were more than skin-deep. With maturity she'd found her own core, her own strength.

Arnie wondered if he had lost more than he had imagined the day Ellie left town.

Chapter Eighteen

The week passed in a blur of grief and a battle to keep emotions in check.

For some, her pastor and her doctor, Vanna's death had not come as a surprise. She'd been born with an enlarged heart. She'd been aware, more than most, that her time on earth would be limited. She'd kept that a secret, a secret that had motivated her to strive as hard as she could to leave a legacy for those who would follow.

To her dismay, Ellie realized she should have recognized the signs of Vanna's impending heart attack—her sickly complexion, the way she rubbed at her jaw and massaged her left arm. If only she'd said something, perhaps Vanna would have avoided, or at least survived, her heart attack.

But Vanna must have known what was coming.

The morning after Vanna's funeral, Ellie was called in to the conference room to meet with the school's board of directors.

Ellie ran a quick comb through her hair, freshened her lip gloss and left her students in Dawn's care.

She shivered a little in the cool, crisp autumn air. Below-freezing temperatures at night and a chill wind had stolen the last of the leaves from the poplar trees that provided a windbreak on the north side of the school property. The branches looked like skeletal hands praying for the quick return of spring.

Taking a steadying breath, she stepped into the main office building. She had no idea why the board wanted to see her and could only hope she wasn't about to be fired.

The board members sat around the same long table where she and the other teachers had met with Vanna so often. They had absorbed her dedication like blotters, had learned the lesson of commitment from her example and were better teachers because of her insights and what she taught.

Richard Connolly, the board president and manager of the local branch of Montana Ranchers and Merchants Bank, stood at the head of the table. He wore a Western-cut shirt with a bolo tie and Western-style dark slacks.

"Thank you for coming, Ms. James," he said. "I know this has been a difficult week for the entire staff, and we appreciate your time."

With a subdued smile, she returned his greeting. She was the most junior of the staff members. If they were going to let her go, she wondered where she'd be able to get another job, particularly at midterm. Would she have to drive all the way to Bozeman? A commute she wouldn't relish.

"I think you know most of the board members," Connolly said. "Arnie O'Brien, of course…"

She'd avoided looking at Arnie, afraid of what she might see in his eyes. But now when his gaze captured hers, she saw a twinkle she couldn't translate and a dazzling smile that set her heart beating double-time. What was he thinking? What did he know?

She'd lost track of Connolly's introductions. Fortunately, she knew Pastor Redmond and recognized most of the other board members, if not by name, by the fact that they had spoken for Ability Counts at both the school board and city council meetings.

Connolly concluded by asking her to sit in the vacant chair at the foot of the table, and she dragged her attention back to the meeting.

"As you may have surmised by now," he said, "Vanna was aware of her heart condition and what it meant for both her future and the future of Ability Counts."

Ellie wondered at Vanna's ability to live her life with the sword of mortality forever poised over her head. An amazing woman.

"In her inimitable fashion, Vanna provided a plan for her own succession and the future of the school," Connolly said. "The board has discussed and evaluated her plan and has agreed with her decision. On Vanna's behalf, we would like to offer you the position of executive director of Ability Counts Preschool and Day Care Center."

His words paralyzed her, and she gaped at the banker in stunned disbelief. Her face flushed, her palms turned sweaty and her ears began to ring. They weren't firing her? They wanted her to take over Vanna's position?

She shook her head. "That's..." Her voice broke. "That's impossible. I'm not qualified—"

"Apparently Vanna thought otherwise." He gave her a fatherly smile, as though she had been named the class valedictorian. "We've examined your record both here and in Spokane. While your experience is limited, we believe, as did Vanna, that you are the best person to carry out the vision of Ability Counts and lead us into the future."

Her mouth had become disengaged from her brain and remained open, but no words were forthcoming.

She cleared her throat. "There are so many things Vanna did for the school that I know nothing about. Fundraising. Architectural drawings. Supervising teachers."

"You're smart, Ellie," Arnie said, still grinning at her. "You'll learn."

"And we'll all be here to help you," the pastor promised.

"Naturally, we can understand if you'd like to take some time to consider our offer," Connolly said. "You have your family to think about and the commitment a position of this nature requires."

"Thank you. As you might guess, I'm beyond surprised." She glanced again at Arnie. Had he known this was coming? If so, he certainly hadn't given her a hint.

The board president walked to her end of the table.

"This is a copy of the contract we'd ask you to sign. You'll notice there would be a substantial increase in your salary and benefits. We're only sorry it can't be more. Nonprofit organizations, as I'm sure you know, operate on a limited budget."

Ellie did know the disadvantages of being a preschool teacher. As director she would have far more financial security, could perhaps have her own place and better insurance coverage for Torie. But she'd miss the day-to-day contact with the children.

She rubbed at her temple as if she could so easily bring order to her confused thoughts.

"Thank you all for this opportunity. I'll give you an answer as soon as I can. Next week at the latest."

Her head reeling, she stood, shook hands with Connolly and headed back to her classroom.

Was she capable of stepping into Vanna's more than capable shoes?

Equally important, was that what she wanted to do with her life?

Vanna had never married, had never had children. Her only family was a sister who lived in Florida. She'd been too ill to come to the funeral.

Ability Counts had been Vanna's family. Her whole life.

Was that what Ellie wanted? She simply didn't know. *Please, Lord, help me. Is this the path You want me to follow? Is this why I was called to return to Potter Creek?*

If she accepted the position, what impact would that have on her relationship with Arnie? Although their relationship already seemed to be at a dead end.

Then again, what had that grin of his meant in the board meeting? That he wanted her to take the job?

Grief was often a passing emotion with young children. That was the case Friday morning, when Ellie set off with her eager students to the O'Brien ranch for their weekly horseback riding class, the last one of the year.

"I bet Daniel will let me ride all by myself," Carson insisted. "He said I'm a real good rider."

"You certainly are," Ellie agreed, glancing into the rearview mirror. "We'll have to see if Daniel thinks you're ready to ride on your own."

"I am," Torie piped up. "I can steer Patches really good."

A tiny barb of panic zinged Ellie's heart. The idea of Torie riding off on her own gave her a good many second thoughts. She hadn't yet recovered from the terror of Torie falling in the river.

The van bumped over the cattle guard and rumbled up the drive toward the barn. Dawn, driving the second school van, followed.

As Ellie parked, she noticed the exterior of Arnie's new house appeared complete, the wood siding gleaming and the windows reflecting the long rays of sunshine.

She hoped Arnie was around this morning. She wanted to talk to him about the job offer and what she should do.

The children bolted out of the van before she could even turn off the engine.

Torie, spotting Arnie coming out of the barn with Sheila, raced toward him. Ellie, her heart soaring at the first sight of Arnie, trailed after her daughter at a more sedate pace.

"Hi, Arnie," Torie said.

"Hey, squirt." He poked a finger in her tummy, making the child giggle. "How're you doing?"

"I'm fine." Torie started to return the poke, but Arnie caught her finger.

"Easy, squirt. My ribs still hurt some."

"My mommy could kiss you and make it all better."

Arnie's rasp of husky laughter set Ellie's cheeks on fire and made her pray the earth would open up and swallow her. She really had to learn to control her reaction to the man. And control Torie's ad-lib comments.

"Maybe another time," Arnie said, winking at Ellie.

Fortunately, Daniel's appearance halted the conversation before Torie could demand more immediate or mortifying action on Ellie's part to reduce Arnie's pain.

The children, including Torie in her most insistent manner, clamored for Daniel's attention, pleading for the chance to ride alone without him or Marc leading the horse.

Without making a commitment one way or the other, Daniel headed for the barn. The children followed close behind, as though on a leash.

Ellie lingered with Arnie. "It seems like I'm always apologizing for my daughter's embarrassing remarks."

"She didn't embarrass me. I thought it was pretty cute."

He would! she thought, mentally rolling her eyes. She folded her arms across her chest, pulling her denim jacket tight. "At any rate, I did want to talk to you about the job offer. If you have time."

"Sure. I think it's a great offer. Wish there was more money on the table, but the board hopes continued fundraising will make that possible."

"I'm not too worried about the salary. It's certainly more than I'm making now. I'm just not sure if I'm right for the job or if I want to make that big a commitment."

He cocked his brow in surprise, took off his Stetson and finger combed his dark hair. "I thought you'd leap at the chance to take over Ability Counts."

"A part of me wants to." She glanced around, then strolled over to the pasture where Daniel's quarter horses grazed, and leaned back against the fence. "I have to think about what's best for Torie. I know Vanna had a lot of evening meetings she had to attend, and she traveled to Bozeman and Helena several times a year. If I took the job, I wouldn't be able to give Torie as much attention as I have been."

He rolled up beside her. "I hadn't thought about that."

"And there's my mother. I think she's coming out of the depression she's had since my dad died, but I hate to make her responsible for Torie all the time. She needs her own friends and activities. Plus, she is getting older."

"Isn't there anyone else you can rely on?"

Ellie gave the question some thought. If Torie had a loving father who was involved in her life, taking on a job like Vanna's might be easier. But that wasn't in the cards for Torie. Or Ellie.

She sighed. "Single mothers have to make a lot of hard decisions and juggle their lives around the needs of their children."

Growing pensive, idly Arnie petted Sheila and stared off into the distance, where two young colts were frolicking in the pasture.

"Guess I hadn't considered that," he said.

"But I have to." She turned to watch the colts with him, wishing she had someone special to rely on. Someone like Arnie.

Somewhere deep in her heart, she'd hoped having this conversation with Arnie would make him realize how much she needed him. How the three of them—she, Arnie and Torie—could be a family.

Tears burned in her eyes. Apparently he didn't believe her love was true enough, strong enough to be worthy of his. Nor, irrationally, despite all evidence to the contrary, did he believe he was good enough to love her?

Her fingers tightened on the top fence rail, splinters rough beneath her palms. She wished someone would knock some sense into the man.

Chapter Nineteen

"I don't think I can accept the job offer."

Pastor Redmond's brows inched upward. Ellie had made an appointment to see him Saturday afternoon in his office. Dressed in a maroon slipover sweater and chinos, he looked much younger than his fifty-some years.

"I'm both surprised and disappointed to hear that," he said. "Can you tell me why?"

"I'm concerned about the amount of time I'd have to be away from my daughter. Being the director is a huge commitment. I'm simply not sure this is the right time in my life to take on that big a job."

The pastor tented his fingers beneath his chin, his hazel eyes gazing at Ellie so intently, she felt a need to squirm in the face of his probing scrutiny.

When she arrived at his office, he'd led her to a grouping of comfortable chairs by the window. A leaf-less poplar tree stood outside on the lawn, the grass turning a golden brown with the arrival of near-freezing temperatures at night.

"When do you think you might be ready to move up into an administrative position?" he finally asked.

Ellie tucked a wayward strand of hair behind her ear. "I'm not sure. My daughter's only five. She won't be in school full-time for two more years. Even then, she'll need child care during after-school hours."

"You live with your mother, don't you?"

"Yes." The promotion would give Ellie a chance to get her own place and at the same time would remove the convenience of having her mother babysit Torie. Yet it wasn't right that she relied so heavily on her mother.

"Tell me…" Still studying her, he leaned back in his chair. "If child care wasn't an issue, would you want to accept the job?"

She chuckled. "In all honesty, the thought terrifies me, but yes, I'd take the job. To make Vanna's vision come to fruition would be an honor, if I could pull it off." She'd never dreamed she'd have that chance. She hadn't sought it. But now that the opportunity existed, she wanted to grab the golden ring.

But did she dare take that big a risk without knowing how it would affect her daughter?

"I can't tell you what your decision should be," the pastor said. "But let's take it to the Lord. The answers we seek are often with Him."

The pastor clasped both of her hands. Together they prayed for the Lord's guidance in the decision she had to make.

When the prayer was finished, Ellie stood. "Thank you for seeing me this afternoon, Reverend."

"Anytime, my dear." He walked her toward the door. "Tell me, how are you and Arnie getting along? I understand you two used to be close."

"Before his accident," she admitted. "I abandoned him when he needed me the most. Now he doesn't trust me, which I can understand. He also believes his injuries make him less of a man, which isn't at all true," she said with a vehemence born of frustration.

"Really? Arnie has always struck me as a strong individual. He's overcome so much."

"I agree, Pastor. He's the only one who thinks of himself as less than he was before the accident."

The pastor's hand rested on the doorknob to the outer office. He tipped his head to the side. "Forgive me for prying, but do you have feelings for Arnie?"

A rush of heat burned her cheeks, giving him the answer to his question. Her throat tight, she whispered, "I never stopped loving him, even though he'd told me to go, to leave him alone. I shouldn't have listened."

"He did?"

"In the hospital. He sounded like he meant it. It broke my heart. So I left and went to Spokane."

"I see." He opened the door for her. "Trust in the Lord, Ellie. He won't fail you."

She could only hope the pastor was right. So far no bolt of insight had struck her about taking—or rejecting—the job offer. She needed to give the board her answer soon.

Right at the moment, her answer would be no.

As for her and Arnie getting together? Even if the Lord and Pastor Redmond intervened, that appeared to be a hopeless cause.

To Arnie's surprise, Pastor Redmond invited himself to Sunday supper at the O'Brien ranch. He'd heard that Arnie had made up a batch of his award-winning chili, or so the reverend had said.

Arnie had the niggling feeling that the pastor had something else on his mind besides a bowl of chili. That feeling grew even stronger when he asked for a tour of Arnie's new house.

"This is terrific!" Pastor Redmond said, standing in the unfinished living room. "You've captured spectacular east and west views with the house placement."

Sheila sat on the floor next to Arnie, her head cocked as she listened alertly to the pastor talking.

"That was the idea. Tim Johnson helped me maximize the layout of the house and the views."

"He's a good man. Honest and hardworking." Hands in his pockets, Pastor Redmond strolled into the kitchen. The pinewood cabinets and granite counters had been installed. Tile floors were going in next week, along with the appliances. Arnie would move into the house before Christmas.

As planned, he'd be moving in alone.

"Did you want to talk to me about something?" Arnie asked, his curiosity getting the better of him.

Turning, the reverend leaned back against the counter. "Tell me what you think of Ellen James."

Arnie blinked and frowned. "I think she'll be a great executive director for Ability Counts. I sure voted for her."

"Yes, you did." Idly, he studied the empty spot where the stove would go. "How about personally? What do you think of her as a woman?"

That niggling feeling Arnie had had all afternoon turned into warning bells. "She's fine," he said with a sharp edge in his voice. "Why do you ask?"

"I was thinking..." The pastor wandered back into the living room. "This is a nice, big house. Three bedrooms, right?"

Arnie nodded.

"That's big enough so a family would be quite comfortable living here. But I don't remember hearing about you dating anyone lately."

Fingers flexing on the armrests of his chair, Arnie said, "Not that it's any of your business, but I'm not exactly an ideal candidate for a husband and father."

"Oh? Because you're paraplegic?"

"Obviously." He bit off the word with a staccato beat.

"That's odd. You're saying none of your paraplegic friends in the Paralympics organization are happily married?"

"Of course they are." They could do what they wanted, but Arnie wasn't going to tie down a woman who, sooner or later, would regret she'd agreed to marry him.

"But you're different. You don't think a woman could love you?" The words were said conversationally, but within them Arnie heard an accusation.

Arnie narrowed his gaze. "What's this all about? Have you been talking to Ellie?"

"We had a conversation," Pastor Redmond admitted. "Mostly about the job offer. She's not sure she'll accept the position."

Arnie hated to think she'd turn the offer down. She'd be good at the job. "You talked about me, too?"

"Some. She thinks you don't trust her."

"I trust her to do a good job as executive director."

"But you don't trust her enough to love her as much as she loves you."

Arnie's breath left his lungs in a whoosh. He wheeled his chair around so he was facing out the window, looking at the pasture with a handful of grazing cows. Not looking at Pastor Redmond.

"She left me once. She didn't stick around when I needed her. If the going got rough, she'd leave me again."

"Do you love her?"

Arnie froze. His jaw tightened. "It doesn't matter."

"Are you sure she left you? Is it possible you sent her away because you were afraid of what had happened to you? Afraid you couldn't handle being disabled?"

"No! She took off without even saying goodbye." *You told her to go. Remember? You were so scared she'd leave you that you beat her to it and told her to go away,* he thought.

How could he have forgotten what he'd done?

The meds. The pain. His head had been so muddled, he could barely remember his name.

The pastor came up behind the wheelchair and put his hands on Arnie's shoulders. "Sometimes the Lord works in strange ways we can't possibly understand. We just have to trust in the path God has given us to follow. That can mean trusting in a good woman's love. And trusting in yourself."

Arnie didn't respond. The weight of Pastor Redmond's words silenced him.

"I imagine you didn't know that Ellie had to go to the head of nursing to get permission to sit with you in the hospital," the pastor said. "The whole time you were in a coma, she barely went home long enough to take a shower and change clothes. That sounds a lot like love to me."

Pain, like a branding iron, burned into Arnie's conscience. "That was a long time ago. Water under the bridge."

"Then, when you began to wake up," the pastor said, ignoring Arnie's comment, "for all intents and purposes, you told her to get lost."

Still standing behind Arnie, the pastor went silent, as though he expected an answer. A defense of Arnie's actions. A defense he didn't have.

Moments later, Arnie heard the pastor cross the floor to the door and pause.

"Sometimes," Pastor Redmond said, "it takes more

courage to love, to take a leap of faith, than to deny that love."

The door quietly closed behind the reverend.

For a long time, Arnie sat staring out the front window as the shadows grew longer. Nausea churned in his stomach. His chest filled with a sea of tears he didn't dare shed.

He'd never really blamed her for leaving. It was the smart thing for her to do. But deep down he hadn't forgiven her, he realized. Had never forgiven her for *not* staying, in spite of having every good reason to leave. *In spite of him telling her to go.*

Sure, he'd gotten on with his life without her. He had the ranch, his cattle, his own house and friends.

Sheila whined and looked up at him expectantly.

"Yeah, I've got you, too, Sheila."

He tried to remember the days right after Daniel had driven them off the road, but the details were blurred. He'd been on heavy pain meds. He vaguely recalled waking up more than once, finding Ellie sitting next to his bed, holding his hand. Talking to him. Then he'd drift off again.

How much time had passed? He had had no way to measure it then and sure couldn't remember now.

Then one day he woke up and she was gone.

He'd lost the one woman he had ever loved.

What a fool he'd been!

Ellie still hadn't told the board her decision, and it was already the middle of the week. The only other time she'd been so unsure of herself was when she left Arnie and went to Spokane.

She'd prayed about the job offer. She'd pleaded for the Lord's guidance.

Silence was the only answer He'd given her.

Working in Vanna's office after the morning preschool session, Ellie sorted through the mail. There were letters of condolence that needed a response, invoices for office supplies that needed to be paid and checks from parents for their children's monthly fees that had to be deposited. Someone had to take care of the routine matters until the decision about a new director was made.

The board was waiting on *her* decision.

"Hey, anybody here?"

Ellie's heart leaped in her chest at the sound of Arnie's voice, and she was unable to tame her sense of joy.

"In here." She pushed aside the paperwork and stood.

Arnie rolled to the office door. His smile and the teasing glint in his eyes nearly undid her.

"There's somebody I want you to meet." He waved in a well-dressed woman in her forties who wore a conservative wool suit and practical heels.

Sheila remained at Arnie's side.

"This is Margaret Metcaf," Arnie said. "She's from the headquarters of the Children's Society in Chicago. She's been in Bozeman this past week, and I asked her to visit Ability Counts." He turned to Ellie. "Ellen James, one of our teachers and likely our next executive director."

Not wanting to correct Arnie's assumption in front of a stranger, Ellie extended her hand. "It's nice to meet you, Ms. Metcaf."

"Please call me Margaret. And I'm delighted to make your acquaintance. For the past two days, Arnie has been talking about nothing but Ability Counts and you. I wouldn't be surprised if your ears had been burning."

Ellie forced a smile. If her ears hadn't been burning before, they certainly were now.

"Margaret does a lot of the society's fundraising, particularly for expansion programs. She's working on developing a network of child development centers across the country."

"I see." Although Ellie wasn't quite sure how that related to Ability Counts.

"Arnie has described Ability Counts and your expansion plans in some detail. I'm quite taken with the model you've developed."

"I'm afraid the credit goes to our founder, Vanna Coulter, who recently passed away." Ellie stepped over to a nearby bookcase, selecting several brochures and the backup material about the school's services. "I can give you some of the materials we've used to describe our plans."

"Thank you. Although I haven't much time—I have to catch a plane back to Chicago in a few hours—I'd like a tour of your facility. If you don't mind."

"It would be my pleasure." She started for the door.

"You see, Arnie has done such a good sales job, I'm thinking our society may want to approach your board with the idea of Ability Counts joining our network of child development centers."

Ellie halted midstride. "Joining?"

"Yes, a shared arrangement under the Children's Society umbrella organization. The local board would still make many of the operational decisions, and we would provide substantial funding to supplement what you raise in your own community."

A wave of dizziness washed over Ellie, and she reached out to steady herself.

Arnie caught her hand. "Now you know why I wanted you to meet Margaret." If possible, the gleam in his eyes had grown even brighter.

"That s-sounds…" Ellie stammered and swallowed hard. "Very interesting."

"Lead on." With a nod, Margaret gestured for Ellie to exit the office first.

In a daze, Ellie showed Margaret the classrooms and discussed the school's educational philosophy. The woman dutifully examined the children's paintings and commented on the layout of the classrooms. She smiled at the day-care students playing outdoors, a mix of disabled children and their able-bodied friends. All laughing. All sharing. Among them there were no differences that mattered.

Some left their playmates to visit with Sheila, who willingly endured their youthful attention.

During the entire tour, Ellie felt Arnie's unceasing attention on her. It was warm and proprietary, as though his hand were resting on the small of her back, directing her. Encouraging her.

Margaret glanced at her watch. "This has been delightful, but if I'm going to catch my plane, I must be going."

"Of course," Ellie said. "Do plan to visit again whenever you're in the area."

"I'm quite sure I'll have that chance, my dear." Margaret bid them goodbye and hurried to her rental car, which she'd parked next to Arnie's van.

Arnie didn't speak until Margaret drove away.

He wheeled his chair around to face Ellie, his expression sober. "So, what do you think?"

"I think it would be amazing if they decide to underwrite Ability Counts." Ellie's fears about her lack of experience at fundraising and leading Ability Counts into the future would be eased. She could handle the teaching and coordinating functions of the director; with luck, over time she'd grow into the rest of the job.

"Ellie, I want you to take the job the board offered you. You're the best person they could hire."

His words and his support warmed her from the inside out. "I still haven't decided." But she was much closer to saying yes.

He glanced around the play yard. "Let's go back inside, where we won't be interrupted. I have something else I want to talk to you about."

Pulling her lip between her teeth, she nodded. Her lungs locked the breath inside her chest; her ears started ringing. Jake had told her they needed to talk and then he'd said goodbye. *No way am I interested in being a father.* He left her on her own to have and raise Torie.

Now she knew… She knew what Arnie was going to say. There was no chance they'd ever be together. He'd taken care of her future. She'd have a decent job. Money enough to raise Torie. Now he wanted to be done with her. Forever.

Her knees trembled with every step she took toward the office. Her shoulders rigid, she walked like a robot. Robots didn't need air. Didn't need love. They simply existed in an emotionless state day after day.

Arnie maneuvered behind her. Urged her to sit in one of the chairs in front of Vanna's desk. She sank onto the leather seat just before her legs gave out entirely.

He took her hands in his. Strong hands callused by the miles, the years, he had had to travel in his wheel-chair.

"I owe you a huge apology, Ellie. If I could get down on my knees to apologize, I would. But I can't do that. I'll never be able to do that."

Her throat tightened. "It doesn't matter." *Nothing matters if you don't love me.*

"I hope you'll always be able to say that." His thumbs stroked lightly across her knuckles. "I've been all wrong about us. I wanted to blame you for leaving me and ignore the fact that I thought that was the right thing for you to do. For your sake. But you came back. And you've been trying to get it through my thick head that you love me."

Unable to hold his gaze, she closed her eyes. "Yes,"

she whispered. If only he'd believe her. If only her love was enough.

"I've finally realized that's all that matters. I can't figure out why you love me. I've been a fool."

A surge of all-but-forgotten hope straightened her spine, and her eyes sprang wide open.

"What I do know is that I love you," he said. "That's what I've been a fool about, denying even to myself that I love you and always have. Always will."

"Oh, Arnie…" Relief ran so deep, it drove the breath from her lungs. Tears blurred her vision.

"If you'll have me—even though I'm not the best candidate for husband of the year—"

"But you are," she protested. "You're a kind, good man. You're brave and honest. You love children and they love you. You're gentle yet strong." She lowered her voice. "Any woman would love you." But none more than Ellie did.

"I want to marry you and love you and take care of you as best I can for the rest of our lives."

"Oh, Arnie…" she repeated. "I love you so much. More than I'll ever be able to tell you."

She leaned forward and he met her halfway. Their lips touched tentatively at first, then with all the emotion that had been bottled up inside for more than eight long years. His were the lips that she had cherished and longed for. His sweet taste fed the yearning she had tried so hard to repress. His special masculine scent filled her with a joy that made her heart sing.

When they broke the kiss, they were both breathing

hard, his pupils so black almost no colour showed in his eyes.

"There is one other thing I need to do before we make this public," he said.

Immediately, she was wary. "What's that?"

He grinned, a lopsided smile that tugged at her heart all over again.

"I have to ask Torie if she'd be okay with me being her daddy."

Ellie tossed her head back and laughed out loud. He'd said he loved her, which she believed with all her heart. But his thoughtfulness of Torie, of taking her wishes into consideration, underscored his love as nothing else could. "I'd say that is a sure thing. She already knows she has you wrapped around her little finger."

"Just like her mother does," he said and kissed her again.

"Should I be asking Sheila if it's all right for me to marry you?" she asked when he finished kissing her.

"I've already had a discussion with her. She said if you turned me down, I'd have to pick up my own dirty socks that I leave on the floor."

Gazing into each other's eyes, they laughed together, the sound of their two voices in perfect harmony with the blessings they had received from the Lord.

Epilogue

Two weeks before Christmas

Ellie and Torie arrived at the hospital labor room a little after 3:00 a.m. They'd almost arrived too late to witness the big moment.

The doctor was already sitting on her stool up between Mindy's legs.

Clothed in a paper gown, Ellie took her place opposite Daniel. She squeezed Mindy's hand.

"You're doing a great job, Mindy," the doctor said. "Let's give her a push now. Make it a good one."

Ellie strained and puffed along with Mindy. Feeling her agony. Knowing her joy. With her free hand, she drew Torie closer to her.

"Here we go," the doctor announced. "Let's take a look…"

Mindy lifted her head.

"Congratulations, Mr. and Mrs. O'Brien. You have a handsome baby boy."

On cue, the baby let out a squall worthy of a cowboy rounding up a herd of beef cattle.

Everyone laughed, and Daniel did the honors of cutting the cord. Then the doctor laid the baby on Mindy's stomach.

"Oh, he's beautiful," she said, tears in her eyes.

Torie tugged on Ellie's paper gown. "Mommy, he's all red and yucky," she whispered.

"You were, too, honey. And I thought you were the most beautiful thing I'd ever seen in the whole world."

"What are we supposed to call him?" she asked.

Ellie looked to Mindy and Daniel for the answer.

"He'll be Robert Daniel O'Brien, named for his grandfather and his daddy," Mindy said. "We'll call him Robbie for short."

Her nose wrinkled, Torie studied the infant until a nurse swaddled him and took him away. She looked up at Ellie.

"I guess Robbie will be okay for a cousin," she said. "But maybe Arnie can help you make a prettier one that's not so squishy and red."

Ellie nearly swallowed her tongue to avoid laughing, but that didn't stop the others. She met Arnie's gaze across the delivery table. His eyes and his teasing smile held the promise of love and laughter that would bind their family together forever. *Thank you, Lord.*

* * * * *

Dear Reader,

I enjoyed returning to Potter Creek and renewing my acquaintance with the local residents. I hope you did, too.

In real life, returning to a community where you once lived may be an eye-opening experience. I remember several years ago I drove by the first elementary school I attended. How did it get so small? I had the feeling someone had slipped the school into an incredible shrinking machine.

Life is filled with changes, some good, some not so much.

I cherish the women I've kept in touch with who were my friends in high school and those I met in my working career. Although we all have acquired more wrinkles, and many of them have experienced heartache, inside they are still the loving, intelligent women I have always admired.

I hope you are blessed with friends like that. Keep them close, for they are the ones who know you best. Happy reading…

Charlotte Carter

Questions for Discussion

1. Do you think Ellie was right to leave Potter Creek after Arnie was injured?

2. Do you think Arnie shared some of the blame for Ellie leaving town?

3. Arnie and his brother, Daniel, are very close now, although they have very different personalities. Are you close to your siblings? What similar traits do you share? What traits don't you share?

4. What might Ellie have missed being raised as an only child? What might she have gained?

5. Are physically handicapped children mainstreamed in your school district? Do you think that's a good idea?

6. What problems and adjustments might a couple face if one of them is paraplegic?

7. Do you read a local paper? What articles interest you?

8. What are the advantages—and disadvantages—of living in a small town like Potter Creek versus a larger city? Which do you prefer?

9. Do you remember attending church picnics as a child? What games did you play?

10. Do you know a single mother? What difficulties and obstacles is she forced to overcome? Are there ways you can help?

11. Women's symptoms of a heart attack are different from those of a man. Ellie witnessed some of Vanna's symptoms of heart disease: apparent pain in her jaw and left arm, paleness and fatigue, sweating. What other warning symptoms might a woman experience? (For information about heart attack symptoms in women visit http://www.heart-attack-symptoms.com/heart-attack)

12. If you were Ellie, how would you have handled Jeffrey Robbins's invitation to dinner?

13. Does anyone you know have a service dog like Sheila? What services does the dog provide?

14. Do you think children as young as Torie should attend the birth of a baby? Why or why not?

INSPIRATIONAL

Wholesome romances that touch the heart and soul.

COMING NEXT MONTH
AVAILABLE NOVEMBER 22, 2011

THE CHRISTMAS QUILT
Brides of Amish Country
Patricia Davids

THE PRODIGAL'S CHRISTMAS REUNION
Rocky Mountain Heirs
Kathryn Springer

HIS HOLIDAY FAMILY
A Town Called Hope
Margaret Daley

THE COWBOY'S HOLIDAY BLESSING
Cooper Creek
Brenda Minton

YULETIDE HEARTS
Men of Allegany County
Ruth Logan Herne

MISTLETOE MATCHMAKER
Moonlight Cove
Lissa Manley

REQUEST YOUR FREE BOOKS!

2 FREE INSPIRATIONAL NOVELS
PLUS 2
FREE
MYSTERY GIFTS